I0682628

MISSION: BETRAYAL

BEAR'S BRIGADE – Book 2

Emily Mims

ALSO BY EMILY MIMS

Bear's Brigade
Mission: Treachery

Durango Street Theatre
Vivi's Leading Man
Maggie's Starring Role
Wade's Dangerous Debut
Jessica's Hero
Letti's Second Act
Cameron Unscripted
Miranda Rewritten
Rachel's Favorite Villain
Sasha's Happy Ending

The Smoky Blues
Mist
Smoke
Evergreen
Indigo
Emerald
Mistletoe
Violet
Ruby
Amethyst
Noelle

The Texas Hill Country
Solomon's Choice
After the Heartbreak
A Gift of Trust

Daughter of Valor
Welcome Home
Unexpected Assets
Never and Always
A Gift of Hope
Once, Again

Other Romances

Season of Enchantment
A Dangerous Attraction
For the Thrill of It All

www.BoroughsPublishingGroup.com

PUBLISHER'S NOTE: This is a work of fiction. Names, characters, places and incidents either are the product of the author's imagination or are used fictitiously. Any resemblance to actual events, locales, business establishments or persons, living or dead, is coincidental. Boroughs Publishing Group does not have any control over and does not assume responsibility for author or third-party websites, blogs or critiques or their content.

MISSION: BETRAYAL
Copyright © 2023 Emily Wright Mims

All rights reserved. Unless specifically noted, no part of this publication may be reproduced, scanned, stored in a retrieval system or transmitted in any form or by any means, electronic, mechanical, photocopying, recording, or otherwise, known or hereinafter invented, without the express written permission of Boroughs Publishing Group. The scanning, uploading and distribution of this book via the Internet or by any other means without the permission of Boroughs Publishing Group is illegal and punishable by law. Participation in the piracy of copyrighted materials violates the author's rights.

ISBN 978-1-957295-41-1

With special thanks to the cops and soldiers who keep us safe

ACKNOWLEDGMENTS

As always, this book was not written in a vacuum. I'd like to thank Boroughs Publishing Group for the superb editing job, and the art department for the hottest cover ever.

MISSION: BETRAYAL

Gypsies, tramps, and thieves
We'd hear it from the people of the town
They'd call us gypsies, tramps, and thieves
— Cher

Chapter One
Preston

Gypsies, tramps, and thieves… Preston wished to hell he could get the damn song out of his head. It had been a fuckin' earworm for the last three days, and he was tired of listening to it.

On the other hand, every single word was accurate. Romani *were* tramps and thieves. If his father told true, one in particular had cost his family a shit pile of money. He wasn't looking forward to the conversation with his father later tonight about the greedy bastard who had stolen almost ten million dollars from their family business. Preston's father was revered in their close-knit Latino community, and he had broken his back to take them from having nothing to where they were now: something Preston was damn proud of despite the fact he wanted nothing to do with the Ramos family business.

He sighed heavily and shifted uncomfortably in the police cruiser. His ass was numb from sitting, and his thermos had run out of coffee. Even though he loved his job as an officer with the San Antonio PD, he could think of more exciting ways to spend the last two hours of his shift.

Unfortunately, kids from a couple of rival high schools had taken to using the wide street he was parked on for late-night drag racing. If it didn't stop, one or more of them were going to get themselves killed.

Unless he was on another call, he'd made it a point to sit here every evening for an hour or two to try to catch the little shits. The fines they were amassing were meant to send a message.

"Tell your friends about tonight," he'd admonish as he handed them the paperwork with a hefty fine. "The drag racing along here stops before one of you end up dead."

The kids would never believe he had a soft spot. No doubt they thought he was an asshole, which was okay. It beat scraping them up off the pavement and having to make a heartbreaking notification to their unsuspecting parents.

He looked at his watch. He had another hour on shift before he could go home to talk with his father about the huge theft from their family business.

"His name's Dominic Kaslov," Roel Ramos had said this morning when he shared the news with Preston. "One of a whole goddamn family of gypsies. They have a history of grifting and thievery going back generations. The bastards are good at it too. Slicker than oil, the whole damn bunch 'a them."

"How much?" Preston had asked through stiff lips.

"The accountant figures it's close to ten million dollars."

Which would hardly break Ramos, Inc., but it was still a helluva lot of money by anyone's standards.

"How'd he do it?"

"A Ponzi scheme with a twist."

He'd heard the whole story about his fuck-up of a younger brother, Jeremy, who'd used company funds, intending to make the company a lot of money. Instead, he'd gotten fleeced.

His father had turned to him with fire in his eyes. "I want you to look into it, boy. Use your connections inside the police department to find out all you can about Dominic Kaslov. Hell, find out what you can about the whole goddamn family. I want to know how we can take them down."

Preston had objected. "That kind of investigation is over my pay grade. You need to swear out a formal complaint and let the detectives look into it. Besides, if Kaslov isn't local, it's out of SAPD's jurisdiction."

"I want you to handle it," his father had insisted. "I don't want it to become public knowledge, which it would the minute I filed a complaint. It would drive down the value of our stock. Find out what you can. See what we need to do and who we need to call in."

Preston supposed he could do that much.

He resumed his radar gun vigil while he used the computer in his cruiser to look up the Kaslov family. He started with Dominic. Hmm. Born in Houston to Romani parents, he'd graduated from a suburban high school. The string of complaints and arrests had begun shortly thereafter.

Surprise, surprise.

Interestingly, none of them were for anything violent or self-destructive. They all seemed to involve creative and illegal ways to get people to part with their hard-earned savings. But there never seemed to be enough evidence to go to trial.

The one time Dominic had been tried, the prosecution hadn't been able to make their case, and the young criminal appeared to have learned nothing from the experience.

From what Preston could tell, Dominic had gone right on with his swindling schemes.

Gullible, naïve Jeremy Ramos, Preston's little brother, had been Dominic's latest target.

Which apparently wouldn't've happened if Preston had done his father's bidding and taken his rightful place as the next head of Ramos, Inc.

He pushed aside the familiar guilt. He'd had no interest or desire to run the company and had never made a secret of it. He hated the business world, and had he done his father's bidding, they would've been at each other's throats constantly.

To his father's everlasting dismay, he'd become a cop. The only time his job had value was when Roel wanted him to "look into" something for him. Which usually meant getting dirt on a business rival. Sometimes Preston deflected the requests, and sometimes, like tonight, his guilt stepped up and he complied.

This time he would do as his father asked. He knew nothing about the Kaslovs in particular, and he hadn't had any personal experience with gypsies. But his mother had.

As a young girl in Fort Worth, she'd seen firsthand the bloody results of a feud between two rival families living in her neighborhood. His father had also experienced a run-in with them a time or two.

From the time he was a child, it'd been drummed into him how sneaky and cunning they were. This business with Dominic Kaslov had not improved his opinion of them one damned bit.

He clocked another speeder at four miles over the speed limit and decided chasing him down wasn't worth the hassle. He continued to research Dominic's family and learned the parents were born in the Balkans and brought their children to the States when they were young. Nothing on the father. Nothing on the mother. A single early arrest for an uncle, but the charges had been dropped, and his record had been clean for over thirty years.

Curious, Preston pushed it back another generation, but he couldn't find anything on the grandparents, other than an ambiguous mention of a group of gypsies trespassing on a farmer's property where a caravan had decided to camp for a few weeks.

Except for the uncle and Dominic, the family appeared to be living within the law. Which wasn't what he expected, and it made him wonder if they really were as law-abiding as they seemed or if they were good at covering their tracks.

He kept looking. Brothers? No. Sisters? Bingo. Sabina Kaslov. Age thirty. Born in Houston. Attended the same high school as her brother. No arrests. Currently stationed at Fort Sam Houston. Another search gave a current address not too far from the base.

A smile crept across his face. How about that. A sibling right here in town. Convenient for a late-night Q and A.

He knew it was a fishing expedition. A long shot. The sister's record was clean, and it was possible she knew nothing about her brother's illegal activities.

Or maybe she was as smart as him and good at keeping things on the DL. Besides, if she was a Kaslov, chances were good she knew something, even if she wasn't an active participant in thieving.

It would be worth a visit to her place to find out.

With his shift finally over, he headed back to his assigned substation. On the way, lights and sirens blazing, he stopped his latest speeder, who turned out to be a terrified young father with his laboring wife in the car. Preston wished them luck and waved the couple on their way.

He took a minute to check on an old homeless man who'd taken up residence in a cardboard box under the bridge and slipped him enough money to pay for some food. He had a soft spot for the old man. For all the homeless in the neighborhood. And he had a real hard-on for the assholes who took advantage of others.

Assholes like Dominic Kaslov.

Rather than changing into street clothes, he stayed in full uniform. A cold February wind plastered his windbreaker to his back as he hiked across the substation parking lot to his truck. It wasn't the most official-looking vehicle, but he'd park it far enough away that Sabina Kaslov likely wouldn't notice.

He'd patrolled her neighborhood some years back and knew it well. He skipped the GPS and headed across town to Sabina's address and found himself faced with a bunch of new apartment complexes that hadn't been there before.

It didn't take him long to zero in on hers, although it took him a few minutes to find the right building with the apartment. He parked around the corner and walked up the flight of stairs leading to her apartment, slowing about halfway up when he spotted a woman in dark clothing in front of the apartment next to hers with a duffle bag at her feet. He watched as she extracted a burglar's tool and started to pop open the door.

"What the hell are you doing?"

"Trying to get into my new apartment. I mislaid my keys." Her voice was husky and low with an accent he couldn't identify.

He raised his eyebrow. "And you just happen to have a set of burglar's tools on you?"

"Part of my job. I didn't want to wake the manager."

"Yeah, right. Let me see some ID."

She shrugged and got out her wallet. His eyes widened, and he had to hold back the shout creeping up his throat. Sabina Kaslov. The sister in question, who he'd caught breaking into her neighbor's apartment. Talk about a lucky break. He could take her downtown for the burglary and quiz her about her brother at the same time.

"Sorry, but I don't believe you," he said. "It looks like you're breaking and entering."

"I'm not," she stated indignantly. "We can straighten this out in five minutes. The manager lives on site. We can walk down to her apartment, and she'll tell you. Show you the paperwork, even."

He shook his head. "Nice try. I caught you in an illegal act. Not a surprise coming from a gypsy."

She went still, and her face darkened. "You have a problem with gypsies?"

He shrugged. "If the shoe fits."

Her eyes widened, her nostrils flaring. "Fuck. You. I'm not breaking into someone else's apartment. If you weren't such a bigot, you'd go downstairs with me, where the manager would straighten this out." She crossed her arms over her chest. "I have someplace I need to be."

"Fine. We'll check with the manager." He marched her down to the apartment she indicated and banged on the door. There was no answer. Preston squared his shoulders. "So much for that diversion. Now we're going downtown."

"Please no. Let me call the manager. I have her number."

He shook his head and called 911 to order a squad car to pick her up. His suspect was looking increasingly upset as he hustled her into the back seat of the squad car.

She got out her phone. "I need to make a call."

He almost let her, then decided, nah, he was perfectly within his authority to hold on to the phone. She might be more willing to talk later so she could make her call.

He plucked the phone out of her hand. "Not until we get to the station, and then not if you give me any trouble."

"You don't understand. I have someplace I need to be tonight. *Please.*"

"No." He turned to the officer driving the cruiser. "Do the chain of evidence for the burglar tools and her bag, and take her downtown. I'll follow you."

He got into his truck, and knowing it would take some time before the evidence was logged, he went through a fast-food drive-through and got a burger, fries, and a shake. He drove to the station and parked across the street in the officers' garage, where he ate his food and sucked down his shake. On his way out of the garage, he waved at the tired-looking duty officer and made his way to the back of the station to the evidence room.

At the counter he signed the paperwork to check the satchel and take her phone—for a change, everything had been processed quickly—and opened the bag. He sucked in his breath. She not only had a set of burglary tools to die for, but all sorts of military-grade spy paraphernalia, as well as a couple of pistols and a dismantled assault rifle.

What the hell? He remembered she was stationed at Fort Sam and thought grunts, especially lady grunts, didn't routinely have this kind of equipment issued to them. He shut the bag and handed it back to the officer on duty in the evidence room, stuffed her phone in his pocket, and went upstairs.

Whatever she was doing in the military, she seemed to be mighty busy in her spare time.

She was seated in an interrogation room and fidgeting with the strap of her handbag, her motions jerky as she muttered under her breath.

He sat across from her and took a moment to look her over. It'd be a stretch to call her beautiful, but she was striking. Her features were bold, her nose and lips prominent. Her dark eyes were framed by dramatic brows, and her complexion was a rich, dark olive. Lustrous black curls framed her face and fell past her shoulders, and what he had seen of her body beneath the dark camo pants and top was muscled, but shapely and appealing.

He could easily imagine her in a long, flowered skirt and revealing top, sitting in front of a crystal ball, telling fortunes while the men in her tribe stole and scammed their way through life.

His lips tightened. "We need to talk."

"I really need to make a phone call," she said. "Please. Then I'll answer any questions you may have."

"You can make the call after we talk." He nailed her with a stare. "You said your tools were part of your job. You're stationed at Fort Sam, right?"

"I am."

"What is a soldier in the United States Army doing with a satchel of tools and weapons?"

"Those are all military issue."

"You need to be more specific."

"It's classified."

"I bet."

"Call the manager. Please. She'll tell you it was my apartment I was trying to get into. Or let me make a phone call. You don't understand what's at stake."

"Oh, I think I do. See, I'm not only interested in what I saw you up to this evening. Tell me, does the name Jeremy Ramos or Ramos Incorporated ring a bell?"

She looked baffled. "No, it doesn't. Should it?"

"It should. It's the company your brother swindled ten million dollars from."

Her gaze zeroed in on his name tag. "And you think I have something to do with it?" Anger flared in her eyes. "You know damned well I wasn't breaking into someone else's apartment. You've got me down here, trying to squeeze information out of me about my brother."

"Ms. Kaslov, you've hit the nail on the head. I want to know exactly what you know about your brother's latest scam."

"Okay." She leaned forward. "I know exactly nothing. Zero. Zip. Goose egg. The last I heard, the little idiot was washing a lot of dirty buildings in downtown Houston. We're not exactly close."

"Surely, you don't expect me to believe you. Gypsy families—"

"Romani," she said.

"Romani families," he hissed as if it burned his tongue, "besides being as dishonest as the day is long, are known for sticking together." She stared at him but remained silent. "Don't look so insulted. You're not the first Romani I've come across, and you won't be the last. Let's try again. What do you know about your brother's most recent criminal activities?"

"Nothing."

He didn't believe her, but she stuck to her story. She crossed her arms. "I'm not answering another question until you let me make a phone call," she said. "We can sit here all night if you like. Or I can ask for an attorney, and you'll be SOL until a public defender shows up sometime tomorrow. But you'll have to charge me first, and we both know you have nothing to charge me with. So, officially, this is an unlawful custodial detention. By law, I can, and will, get up and leave right about now."

Well, fuck him.

He handed her the phone.

She turned away and spoke quietly and urgently to a "colonel."

Probably the nickname of a fellow criminal.

She hung up and dropped the phone into her handbag, and he wiggled his fingers for her to hand it back, which she did.

"Now, where were we?"

"You were asking me questions I don't have the answers to."

"See, that's where we differ. You've made your phone call. Start telling me what you know."

She shook her head tiredly. "I'm doing you a solid by not walking out and jamming you up. Believe it or not, officer, we're on the same side.

"Now, I've told you I don't know more times than is necessary. I'm not going to sit here and tell you my brother's lily white, because I know he's not. But it has nothing to do with me. Nothing."

"What about the rest of your family? Are they into the same crap your brother's into?"

"No."

"Come on. I don't believe you for a minute."

"I don't expect you to. We're used to prejudice."

"You know what? I can think of maybe ten million reasons that might be true." He was about to press further when night sergeant Bud Shipley snapped the door open and strode inside.

"Ms. Kaslov, you're free to go. I apologize for the inconvenience, ma'am."

Preston reared back. "*What*? I don't think so."

"I said she was free to go," Bud reiterated, pissed and not looking like he was trying to hide it. He handed her the satchel and turned to Preston. "Give her the phone."

She held out her hand, and he slapped the phone into her palm. She turned to Bud. "Thank you. I'll need a ride to my car."

"Officer Ramos can take you."

She looked at him and shook her head. "Can someone else take me? At this point I don't trust Officer Ramos to get me there. He seems to have some issues concerning Romani in general, and me and my family in particular."

Preston felt the flush creep up his neck from anger and embarrassment.

"Of course," Bud said. "I'll have one of the other officers drive you."

She turned to go.

"This isn't over, Ms. Kaslov," Preston said quietly. "I'll be keeping an eye on you."

She shrugged and walked out.

He opened his mouth, but Bud beat him to it. "What the hell was that all about? I had three calls in ten minutes, including one from some big-shot colonel and one from a pissed-off general. The one who's in command of Fort Sam Houston, and he was raising all kinds of hell because you detained her without cause.

"They both said you could've verified her story within five minutes, and she could've been on her way. Instead, you hauled her down here and badgered her for the better part of an hour. She was part of something important, and you messed it up royally. Care to tell me what that was all about?"

"Her brother swindled ten million from my dad's company. I wanted to find out what she knows. And she knows something. I guarantee it. I think it was worth a couple of hours to find out what."

"Maybe she does, maybe she doesn't. Damn it, boy. You're too close to the matter to be questioning anyone about it. And, because of your stupidity, you brought down the wrath of the fucking U.S. Army on us tonight.

"Got news for you, asshole. You may've thought it was worth the time, but they didn't, and they're as pissed as all get-out. You understand what that means for you? For the SAPD?"

Preston understood completely.

He just didn't give a fuck.

Chapter Two
Sabina

Sabina sat beside her commanding officer as he fought his way through the late afternoon traffic into downtown San Antonio. Their detachment had gotten home from the FUBAR mission two days ago, and the entire team was furious at the tragic outcome. An outcome that could've been prevented but for the two-hour delay caused by Sabina's detainment by Officer Preston Ramos.

Sabina still shook with rage when she pictured the three executed hostages they'd found in the Mexican hut, one a beautiful eight-year-old boy. It had taken two days and the threat of a government lawsuit to arrange this meeting with the San Antonio Police Department, one that would include the Chief of Police. Base commander, General McKinley, had insisted on it.

"Chief Dekker needs to know the kind of prejudice and preconceptions his officers are carrying in the workplace," he'd said to Colonel Bear Bustamante, Sabina's OIC, who, in turn, had told her. "It needs to be addressed, starting with the officer who detained Sergeant Kaslov."

So here they were, on their way downtown, hoping to right a wrong. "I'm dreading this, sir," she said as the colonel braked for a light.

"I know, Sergeant. But every one of us, from the general down, is ready to nail the asshole to the wall. There was nobody who could go in your place, and the bastard cost three people their lives. The asshole needs to pay."

Sabina huffed. "He thinks my brother swindled his family out of a lot of money, and he's convinced I know what's going on. My question is, how does a street cop's family have that much money? I think he's lying about the amount."

"Maybe not if his family are the Ramoses in Ramos, Inc. It's one of the most successful Latino businesses in San Antonio. They have considerable business dealings on both sides of the border."

"I wonder why he's a cop."

"Don't know. Maybe he doesn't like the business world. Or he has a need to wear a gun and feel like he's in charge. Some cops do, as do some soldiers."

"I'm afraid he's going to harass me again. His parting shot was that he intends to keep an eye on me."

The colonel raised a brow. "Is it possible your brother is responsible?"

"Dominic is capable of all sorts of illegal schemes. But I'm not guilty of anything, and neither is anyone else in the Kaslov clan.

"Mom's family went straight when they came here. It was a new start for them, a new way of living. Maybe Dad's family wasn't as squeaky clean. Uncle Milo pulled a thing or two as a young man, but Mom's parents were living honestly, and they told Dad he'd have to do the same if he thought to marry Mom. They gave up their former lifestyle and live like *gadgo*."

"*Gadgo?*"

"Non-Romani. Mom's a school secretary. Dad sells real estate. No caravans and nothing dishonest. They encouraged us to get educations and to make friends with everyone, Romani and *gadgo* alike."

"Do they condone your brother's behavior?"

"No, they don't. But they've been known to cover for him. Not so much because we're Romani and they don't want his crap to stick to us. It's because they love him and want to protect him. Not that it really seems to make much difference to him. He does what he does, and if it screws with the family, he's immune to the effects of his behavior.

"Typically, when people find out we're Romani, they assume we're grifters, dishonest, and out to steal a buck. Dominic's behavior feeds into the stereotype."

"The stereotype the officer alluded to."

"Stereotypes are pervasive and damned hard to overcome. Even after taking the mandatory bias training class, a lot of the soldiers can't shake them off."

"Don't I know it. Things are way better than when I started. I still get pissed when I remember the old master sergeant who told me as a young lieutenant I should be proud of myself since I was a credit to my race. After all, most Meskins were dumb and lazy."

Sabina winced. "He got away with that?"

"I chewed his ass out for all the good it did. He was retiring, and I was delighted to see him go. His attitude wouldn't be tolerated today, especially with my team. As you know, we've got a little bit of everyone in Bear's Brigade."

"We do, don't we?"

"Sad thing is no one's immune. You ought to hear the stuff we review at command level.
There are old timers who are stuck in the past and some assholes who will always have a bias against some or many groups. In any case, there's no place for that in the military."

"And in civilian life. I can only imagine what Dr. Castillo puts up with, being a beautiful and talented Black woman and a Latina."

"Yeah, and thanks." The colonel smiled.

His new girlfriend was the all-around best, and the team was so happy he'd found her. These days, he was a lot less cranky than he used to be.

Sabina's tension ratcheted up when the colonel pulled into the parking lot across the street from the downtown station. They entered the sleek new headquarters and showed their IDs to the officer staffing the desk. He checked his computer and told them,

"Go up to the fourth floor to conference room four twenty-five. The elevators are just beyond the doors." He buzzed them in and locked the doors behind them.

The conference room was about halfway down a long hall. They stepped inside, and Sabina stiffened at the sight of a clearly angry Officer Ramos sitting between two officers in plain clothes with badges clipped to their jacket pockets.

Chief Dekker, dressed in his SAPD uniform, sat at the head of the table.

Sabina was glad she and the colonel were also in uniform. Their DCUs were a subtle message: they weren't intimidated by the uniforms worn by members of the SAPD and could out-badass the officers in their sleep.

The chief motioned to two empty chairs, and they sat. Sabina sneaked a look at Officer Ramos while the police chief made a production of looking through his notes.

Nope. No change. Ramos wore the same expression she'd encountered the other night. Same granite-carved face, well-formed and appealing, despite what she suspected was a constant scowl.

His features were like the conquistadors she'd seen in old paintings: prominent cheekbones in a tanned face; a long, strong nose; and lush lips. His hair was straight and dark, and his eyes were a deep brown. Almost as dark as hers. His jawline was square, maybe more so today as he seemed to be clenching his teeth.

She was glad he was pissed off and probably aggravated. If this meeting went the way her commander wanted, the asshole would be even more enraged when it was over.

The chief made quick work of introductions. The suit on Officer Ramos's left was introduced as Louis Farrar, Head of Internal Affairs, and the bulldog-looking man on the right was Ramos's union rep, Jack Patoski.

The chief glanced down at his notes, then cleared his throat. "The Army has brought to the attention of the department that Sergeant Kaslov's rights were violated, and she was detained unnecessarily by

SAPD Officer Preston Ramos." He added the time and date. "I received formal complaints from General Amos McKinley, the head of Army South at Fort Sam Houston, and General Tom Beecher, the base commander. Hence the meeting this afternoon."

"If I may," Patoski interjected.

"No, sir, you may not," the chief said curtly. "You'll have a chance to speak on Officer Ramos's behalf later. I've read your report. I've also read the officer's report, as has Lieutenant Farrar, as have you. Officer Ramos, is this an accurate reflection of the incident involving Sergeant Kaslov?"

"It is," Ramos said tightly.

Chief Dekker handed Sabina and Colonel Bustamante a copy of the report. "Please look this over, Sergeant, and tell us if it squares with your memory of the incident."

Sabina took her time reading over the document. "No, it doesn't. Not at all. There are significant omissions."

"I don't think—" Patoski again interrupted.

"Mr. Patoski, I've asked you to be quiet," the chief snapped. "You'll get your opportunity to speak later." He turned to Sabina. "What kind of omissions?"

"There's much made in the report about my suspicious behavior regarding the supposed break-in. Once we were downtown, Officer Ramos spent all his time questioning me to the point of harassment about my brother's suspected criminal behavior, even though I repeatedly told him I knew nothing about Dominic's criminal activities regarding the Ramos family or the Ramos corporation. He even admitted that was why he'd taken me in. To question me about Dominic. That's barely touched on in the report." She took a breath. "He also made mention of the fact that we're Romani. Gypsy, I think he called it. He seemed to think this was in and of itself an indictment. That I was doing something wrong because of my heritage. That's not dealt with at all in this report."

The chief's eyes widened. "Officer Ramos?"

"Family members are frequently questioned regarding a suspect," Patoski said smoothly.

Ramos looked defiant. "Her brother swindled ten million from my father's company. Getting to the bottom of a theft like that is worth an hour of her time."

"Are those family members hounded and harassed in the manner that she was?" Colonel Bustamante broke in fiercely. "Are they hauled downtown and refused a phone call that could have cleared this up in five minutes? Do you routinely take care of family investigations while you're off duty and still in uniform, which is questionable in and of itself?" He looked over his copy. "Also, I see no mention of Sergeant Kaslov being made aware of her rights. Was she?"

"She was never under arrest," Ramos said tersely. "As far as the phone call goes, it was my decision if and when to let her make her call. I didn't have to let her call at all, and most officers wouldn't have."

"Besides, she could have asked for an attorney at any time," Patoski added.

"Actually," the colonel said, "Sergeant Kaslov told Officer Ramos that she knew she wasn't under arrest and was being unlawfully detained. As such, she could have left at any time without Officer Ramos's consent. Had he allowed her to make her phone call when she first requested, the matter would've been resolved in five minutes, and she could have been on her way. That didn't happen, because Officer Ramos had an axe to grind, which was inappropriate, and based on his inherent bias."

"I didn't ask for an attorney because of the time factor in getting one," Sabina said. "I thought, mistakenly, if I answered his questions, he'd let me go quickly."

"What it boils down to is that she was taken down here and hassled," Colonel Bustamante said, "for what amounted to hours, and that had dire consequences for an assignment the sergeant was to have carried out that evening."

"An assignment that involved a satchel full of burglar tools?" Patoski broke in.

"As a matter of fact, yes." The colonel's voice was even, but his eyes sparked. "The tools were issued to her by the Army and are part of her job."

"You mind telling us what kind of assignment?" Patoski pressed.

"It's classified. That's all you need to know," the colonel shot back.

"None of which is relevant," Patoski said dismissively.

"What's relevant is your cop screwed up," the colonel snarled.

"It was relevant enough I got phone calls from the two highest-ranking officers on the base," Chief Dekker reminded them. "And Colonel Bustamante is here with the sergeant this afternoon. I think that makes it relevant, Mr. Patoski."

The chief turned to Sabina. "Is there anything you can add about your brother, Sergeant?"

"No."

"Do you honestly expect us to believe that?" Patoski challenged. "Romani families are notoriously close."

"And that means?" the colonel asked.

"That they cover for each other," Patoski answered.

The chief and the internal affairs officer seemed taken aback.

The colonel raised his brow. "More prejudice on the part of SAPD?"

"Absolutely not. It's the truth." Patoski looked indignant.

"Sure sounds like prejudice to me." Colonel Bustamante scowled and folded his massive arms across his chest.

Sabina leaned forward. "Like all families, there are some people within them who chose a criminal path. If blood relation was the basis for finding people guilty, three quarters of the people who live in Texas would be in prison. My family's heritage, and the bias surrounding that heritage, makes us targets and is why I find the officer's remarks so offensive."

"What exactly were those remarks?" Farrar from Internal Affairs asked. "What did the officer say to you?"

"That we are dishonest and we always stick together. That my family is into the same crap as Dominic, and he didn't believe me when I said we weren't. That since I was 'gypsy,' I was pre-destined to commit crime. He also threatened me. Said he was going to keep an eye on me from now on. His report made no mention of the slurs he spewed and barely touched on the threat."

Chief Dekker turned to Ramos. "Do you have any explanation for these omissions?"

The officer's face turned a deep shade of red. "I didn't find them important."

"Seems you were trying to cover your unfortunate behavior." Colonel Bustamante sneered. "Falsifying a report. That's illegal."

"It's not falsified."

"Completely untrue," Sabina shot back.

"I didn't falsify anything. I didn't report what was said word-for-word. There's a difference, and you both know it. The gist of what was said is there. Furthermore, it's still my contention her brother swindled money from my family," Ramos said tightly. "I was trying to find out what, if anything, she knew."

"Officer Ramos acted within the law," Patoski added. "He's a fine officer, and we're proud to have him in the department."

Colonel Bustamante slapped the table hard. "An unlawful detention. Harassment. Ethnic slurs. And threats. Glossing over the truth on an official police report. Pursuing a private matter for his family while wearing an SAPD uniform. If he's an example of a fine officer, I'd hate to meet one of your crappy ones."

The colonel didn't try to hide his anger. "I'm not a lawyer, but your officer abused his authority. What he did doesn't sound legal or ethical, and every one of you sitting here at this table knows it. He was way out of line. If a military cop acted like your officer did, he'd lose his position and might be kicked out of the service so fast it would make your head swim."

He leaned forward. "The only reason Sergeant Kaslov and I are here and not getting half the lawyers in the JAG office to file a legal complaint on her behalf is that national security is involved, and there's a need for secrecy. I'm sure your department would like to keep it that way, because the alternative is an avalanche of alphabet agencies coming through your doors asking questions. Questions that could land the department in a world of hurt. Questions that would be featured on the evening news and give your department a huge black eye."

"We'll conduct an internal investigation," Farrar said quickly.

"And you'll cover up everything. Officer Ramos will get a slap on the wrist and will have learned nothing," the colonel said. "Lieutenant Farrar, you don't need to conduct some bullshit investigation. You know everything you need to. As does the chief. Officer Ramos acted outside his authority as a police officer and displayed a serious ethnic bias your department needs to address. Detaining my sergeant under false pretenses had serious and unfortunate consequences. I want to know exactly how you intend to address it."

Farrar glared at the colonel, and Sabina thought, *Wrong guy to try to stare down.*

"Remember, I report directly to both those generals who are quite unhappy," the colonel continued. "If they don't get some satisfaction from what transpires today, they'll be calling in those alphabet agencies, and the first door they will be knocking on is yours. After a visit with Chief Dekker, that is."

They all sat silently for a long moment as the very real threat sunk in. "All right. The Army has a point," Chief Dekker said. He took a deep breath. "How can the department make this right?"

"Fire the officer," Colonel Bustamante said bluntly. "Make him an object lesson to your department."

Sabina bit her tongue and tried not to quirk her lips in satisfaction as Ramos sucked in his breath.

"That would require a hearing, which will likely result in more publicity than you want," Chief Decker said slowly. "But we are willing to take other appropriate action."

"Okay, then. You can start with sending the officer for intense bias training as well as a thirty-day suspension without pay," the colonel said.

Patoski started shaking his head. "You can't come in here—"

"Consider it done." The chief faced Ramos. "Turn in your badge and your weapon to your sergeant on your way out."

Ramos turned his head in Sabina's direction. Sabina swallowed. If looks could kill, she and the colonel would be dead.

"Thank you," the colonel said. "That's a start."

"A start?" Patoski said.

"Remember, the suspension is his punishment, but it's going to do little or nothing to address the cause of the incident, which is the blatant prejudice held by Officer Ramos against those of the Romani community," the colonel said. "It's clear his bias runs deep, and his behavior isn't likely to change with punishment alone. The Army offers excellent classes on identifying and dealing with bias. Officer Ramos could benefit from the training. I suggest he, and perhaps others in your department who've exhibited bias or insensitivity, take the course taught by Sergeant Kaslov. I'm sure she would be delighted to offer this training to your officers."

Chief Dekker turned to her. "I'm sure our officers would benefit from your training."

Sabina was torn between laughing and shuddering. On the one hand, talk about just desserts. But, in actuality, she wouldn't be delighted to teach a bunch of narrow-minded, prejudiced cops, especially this asshole. Even if they would benefit from the instruction. But to show cooperation, she inclined her head. "It would be my pleasure."

They agreed on a time and a place after Ramos returned to duty. The chief turned to Farrar. "Look through your files and flag any officers who've had incidents in the last two years. Choose those you think will benefit from the training. I trust you'll be open to it, Officer Ramos. I expect to see positive changes in the department come from this unfortunate incident."

The officer nodded wordlessly.

"Then I believe we're done here." Colonel Bustamante stood up, and they all rose with him.

Ramos glanced over at Sabina with rage in his eyes. "Officer Ramos," she said quietly. He turned to face her. "You promised to keep an eye on me. You'll have an easier time of it now." She ignored his gasp of outrage. "Have a good evening."

The chief and Farrar watched the officer stomp out.

"Touché, Sergeant." The colonel's eyes danced. "Come on. The generals are waiting for me to brief them."

They wasted no time getting back to base. The colonel dropped her beside her three-year-old Camaro in the instructors' parking lot. A cold February drizzle sparkled on her windshield as she headed the few blocks to her new apartment.

The apartment for which she now had multiple spare keys.

Ramos was a good-looking bastard, she thought with chagrin as she idled at a light. A little old for her thirty years. The faint lines at the corner of his eyes and the gray sprinkled at his temples said late thirties, perhaps forty. But he was still visually appealing if nothing else.

Which was a crying shame.

He was the best-looking, sexiest man she'd come across in a long time.

But he was a grade-A, first-class asshole.

The light turned green, and she gunned the engine, eager to get home out of the cold. With his family's money, he probably wouldn't even miss the month's salary. Even if he did, nothing would ever make up for little Kieran Lavigne, his beautiful mother, and aunt—all shot dead because her team didn't get there in time to save them because Ramos was dicking with her downtown over something her brother may have done.

An asshole, plain and simple. No two ways about it.
But then, the gorgeous ones always were.

Chapter Three

Preston

Preston parked his car at the Northside Substation and hustled to the front door. Last week's spitting rain had turned into this week's sleet, and San Antonio drivers had spent the day trying to negotiate icy roads while sliding into one another. He'd half expected to get a phone call telling him he should come back to work. His suspension was up tomorrow, but the phone had been irritatingly silent. Instead, he'd spent the afternoon painting the hall bathroom in the fixer-upper in the Deco District he'd bought after his divorce. The house was nearly a hundred years old and had been neglected for years, but it had what his mother called "good bones," so he was slowly restoring it to its previous glory.

Preston thought of the house with satisfaction. It was exactly the kind of house his ex-wife hated. She'd insisted they purchase a turnkey in the newest subdivision on the far north side of town. "You're still a Ramos," she'd chided every time he complained about the tacky McMansion. "Even if you refuse to be part of the family business." She'd spent the better part of the five years they were married trying to persuade him to quit the department and go to work for his father.

They were both relieved when she finally gave up and filed for divorce. The first thing he did when the divorce was final was sell the McMansion and use his half of the proceeds to buy his fixer-upper. Besides appealing to him aesthetically, working on it was terrific stress relief.

He'd done *a lot* of work on it in the last month.

But it had done little for his stress. Or his burning anger at Dominic and Sabina Kaslov. He wasn't happy with the Army, either. He'd never realized how much clout the fat cats at Fort Sam had in the civilian community.

Mostly, though, he was unhappy with himself. He'd been out of line. Hell, he'd been a real shit to her, letting his prejudice rule his actions that night, which had given the department the black eye from hell from the Army, and his behavior nearly cost him his job.

He was sure as hell paying the price.

He should've gritted his teeth and kept his mouth shut regarding his opinions about the Romani community.

Actually, he should've never tried to track her down in the first place.

He'd have liked to blame his father for laying the guilt on him, but it was his fault for acting on the out-of-line request.

Preston knew better than to use his badge for personal or family reasons.

Once inside, he said hello to the desk sergeant, an old friend from his rookie days, and ambled down the hall to the meeting room where the class was being held. He sat about halfway from the front and pulled out his iPad. The whole thing was a crock, but if the department wanted him to take the course as a form of penance, so be it. Still, it chapped him he had to take the course from the woman he still had doubts about.

Besides, something more was going on with her. No way did two generals get involved in an inconsequential detainment of a Fort Sam soldier. What happened sure as hell shouldn't've triggered the backlash it did. Or the punishment he'd received.

He was beginning to wonder what pile of Army shit he'd managed to step in.

And the cherry on the cake? His dick got hard every time he thought about her, which pissed him off big-time.

His mood took a deeper dive when Officer Aaron Crowley sauntered into the room. The asshole had to be the biggest racist in the department, having a strong opinion on everyone who wasn't a white, heterosexual male like him. You name 'em, Crowley had contempt for 'em. He'd had more than one run-in dealing with the public, and it had gotten to the point most of the department, Preston included, would duck behind a door to avoid having to interact with the motherfucker.

A smile played around his lips. He could hardly wait to see Crowley tangle with Sergeant Kaslov. Too bad there wasn't a bet pool going. He'd put his money on Crowley and make a killing.

One by one the rest of the officers assigned to take the course wandered in. Preston looked around at his classmates. Mostly older, with a few younger cops known for having a bad attitude. Ethnically it looked like a cross-section of the department: white, brown, and black.

There were only a couple of women. He didn't know everyone here, but the ones he did know he didn't like. *For the very reason they're here with me this evening.* They weren't the nicest people in the department. Far from it.

He looked around again with a feeling of chagrin and, perhaps, a little guilt at being included in *this* group.

The officers sat sullenly for the most part. At the stroke of nineteen hundred, Sergeant Kaslov, in freshly ironed DCUs, strode in with a laptop and a small portable speaker. She pulled down the screen and quickly set up the laptop and speaker.

She looked around at the assembled officers, seeming to making eye contact with each of them one at a time.

"Good evening. I'm Sergeant Sabina Kaslov, currently stationed at Fort Sam. Tonight we're beginning a four-week study of prejudice and bias. Otherwise known as the 'I-don't-like-them-bastards' course."

Her expression remained neutral as a few people snickered. Most looked at her uncertainly.

"That's right. Among other things, we're going to examine the us-versus-them mentality that is the root of all prejudice and examine ways to recognize it and mitigate its effects when dealing with others."

"You really think you can teach us all not to be prejudiced?" Crowley drawled.

"No. Your prejudices are your own and probably so deep-seated they can never be eradicated. But I can teach you ways to recognize those prejudices so that you can put your bias aside and deal with people fairly."

Another hand shot up. "What if I don't want to?" one of the younger cops asked.

"Don't want to what? Deal fairly with the people you're being paid to serve and protect? The people whose tax dollars pay your salary? Then I guess your ass stays in trouble until the department finally has had enough and gives you the boot. Or until you pull a really good one and end up going to prison for a few years."

Sergeant Kaslov looked around the room, her expression solemn. "It's twenty twenty-three, people. The era of cell phones and body cams. You're accountable for everything you do. You beat on anyone and it shows up on the internet in real-time. The news cycle picks it up within the hour, and if not immediately, eventually, you get charged with assault.

"You insult somebody's grandma, her son, who happens to be an attorney, is down here the next afternoon filing a complaint. You use a racial slur during an investigation, you get called out onto the carpet."

You jack around with a Fort Sam soldier, the Army brass gets your ass suspended for thirty days.

Yeah, yeah, Preston got the point.

"You can't get away with stuff you could have fifteen or twenty years ago." Sergeant Kaslov gave it a moment to sink in. "But bias also works the other way too. How many of you have let a pretty woman off with a warning when anybody else would have gotten the ticket? Or let an offense slide because the old lady reminded you of your grandmother? Or changed your mind about arresting the DUI because his brother's an old friend of yours?

"Sometimes we don't even realize we're doing it. Bias is pervasive throughout our society. Let's spend a few minutes looking at how."

She lowered the lights and fiddled with something on her laptop. The screen lit up, and Cher's voice blasted into the room. "Gypsies, tramps, and thieves…"

Damn. He'd just shaken off the earworm, and now it was back.

They listened to the first verse and the chorus before the video switched to Mick Jagger singing *Brown Sugar*. Then a Frito Bandito ad popped up, and then Ashton Kutcher in brownface.

The inevitable ads about technology so simple a woman could handle it. Elton John singing *Island Girl*. A panda selling bamboo furniture. A Black family eating fried chicken. A blouse ad with a white girl on the arm of a Mexican in a sombrero. *Kung Foo Fighting*. Cher again, singing *Half-Breed*. Movie posters for *Mandingo*, *Song of the South*, and *Gone with the Wind*. And so on.

The video ran for about ten minutes. "Pervasive, isn't it?" Sergeant Kaslov said. "And we didn't even get to the shirtless SEALs in the romance aisle."

This time the class laughed.

Now she had their attention, Sergeant Kaslov went on to talk about the differences between overt racism, which she said was openly expressed, and covert, which could be so subtle people didn't recognize it, even in themselves.

She addressed the us-versus-them mentality that spawned prejudice before handing out pieces of paper with a column of descriptors, like "Black man," "single mother," and "white policeman."

"This evening we're going to talk about overt racism. Write down your first impression when you read the word. Be honest, not politically correct."

Preston hid a smile. Politically correct? This bunch? She had to be kidding.

"You have five minutes."

They bent their heads and started writing.

Preston went down the list, growing more interested by the descriptor. Every one of them was going to be a trigger for somebody. He answered as best he could, wondering if he would find gypsy on the list. Sure enough, there it was, about two-thirds of the way down. He skipped it and went on to the next one. She knew what he thought about gypsies, and he knew she knew.

It would be interesting to see if anyone else shared his prejudice.

He'd barely finished when she called time.

"Now, let's talk about some of these," Sergeant Kaslov said. "Were any of them triggers for you? Black man? How about some of you tell us what you wrote?"

Rapper. Perp. Lowlife. Daddy. Football coach. Neighbor. Preacher. It seemed everyone had a trigger of some sort.

Sergeant Kaslov asked the group how they believed these perceptions might affect an officer's dealings with a young Black man at a traffic stop. "How will realizing a potential prejudice affect how you treat him? Or will it?"

Most agreed it should make a difference but admitted changing their behavior wouldn't be easy. They went on to some of the other words. The associations were interesting. What one person found favorable, another sitting next to him viewed entirely differently. The exchanges tended to be lively. Crowley and one of the women nearly came to blows over "single mother."

"We're not whores, we're providers," the woman snapped. She turned to Sergeant Kaslov. "You need to add redneck to your list, so I can write down asshole."

The sergeant neatly defused the situation and carried on.

As the class progressed, Preston had to admit she made a lot of good points, reminding the class that while they were biased against others, others were also biased against them: as police officers, as members of their ethnic group, as whatever.

She was right. He thought of all the times he'd been accused of playing at his job because his family was wealthy.

Bias was pervasive throughout society, and he'd been as guilty as hell of it in dealing with her. But he was still convinced her brother was guilty of swindling his little brother, and he wasn't entirely convinced the rest of her family had gone straight, even though nothing had turned up on them. If that made him prejudiced, then he guessed he was prejudiced, though it stung him with a twinge of guilt.

She thanked them all for coming. "I'll see you all next week."

He headed for the door and was halfway to his car when his phone buzzed, and he saw a text from his mother.

I saved you a bowl of carne guisada if you want to come by for a late dinner.

It for sure beat the leftover takeout Chinese from last night, even if it did mean dealing with his father.

Preston headed out for the upscale condo his parents moved to a few years ago and took the elevator to their spacious fifteenth floor unit.

His mother greeted him at the door with a hug. "Come on in. I saw your truck pull in the parking lot and put your dinner in the microwave. Your father's in the living room."

"Enjoying the view, no doubt." The condo had views looking in three directions, all of them prettier at night than in the daytime. His mother headed for the kitchen, where he found his father with his feet propped up and a bottle of his beloved Tecate in his hand.

Preston grinned crookedly. Roel Ramos might be rich with a fancy condo and a top-of-the-line Lexus, but he still loved the beer of his youth, when he'd been a poor kid growing up on the wrong side of the tracks in Laredo.

He'd done his best to raise his sons as children of privilege, with Preston destined to take over his extensive business holdings, and Jeremy as Preston's right-hand man.

But Preston had rebelled. Instead of the MBA his father had wanted him to get, he'd received a criminal justice degree, and after a stint in the Army, went to work for SAPD.

Reluctantly, Jeremy had taken Preston's place, but he cared little for the business and had no head for it, as this latest incident proved.

Roel Ramos's sons were deep disappointments to him, and he let them know it loudly and often.

His father looked up as he stepped in and sank down in one of the easy chairs. "Still in the doghouse at work?"

Preston rolled his eyes. "I went to the first bias training class tonight. Mom took pity on me and offered me dinner."

His father swallowed a mouthful of beer. "Was it as much *tonterías* as you expected?"

"Bullshit?" Preston raised his shoulders slightly. "Some of it was good. Some of it I could've done without. What she didn't address was how you're supposed to be unbiased and fair when somebody's robbed you blind."

"Like Dominic Kaslov."

"Like Dominic Kaslov."

"None of which made a bit of difference when the Army was throwing its weight around. I wonder what they would do if I decided to throw my weight around too," Roel mused.

Preston sighed. "Please don't. They already think I'm a spoiled rich boy at Daddy's beck and call, and they resent the hell out of it, which may be part of why the chief went along with the colonel's suggestion and suspended me. It's not the first time I've brought a Ramos, Incorporated problem to the job, and they know it."

"Tough. What's the point of having a son on the police force if I can't take advantage of it every so often?" His father paused a minute. "What do you think? The woman's telling the truth? Have the rest of them really gone straight?"

"I don't see how. Maybe she has. She's got security clearance, but I wouldn't put it past the rest of the family to still be in the life, at least to some extent. The uncle has an old arrest record. I don't know if they're really honest or fucking smart."

"Smart. Definitely smart."

"Speaking of smart, why did Jeremy fall for the scam in the first place? How did it get past him? Those documents you showed me had red flags all over them even before you said it was all bogus."

Roel's lips tightened. "Your brother not only lacks a head for business, but he's naïve in the extreme. Naïve and trusting, and sometimes I don't think he's overly bright. But no matter. He'll have to learn. At some point I'll need to turn the company over to him. Naïve or not, he's the only one who can take it over."

"He doesn't have to run it. Sell it to someone who can."

"Fuck that. I will do no such thing. Jeremy will run it. Since you won't." He glared at Preston. "If you'd take your place in the company, none of this would be an issue."

"Not gonna happen, and you know it. Even if I wanted to step in, I know jack shit about business and don't feel like starting over at thirty-eight. You'd be better off selling it when the time comes or hiring somebody who knows what they're doing. In the meantime, we do what we can to bring Dominic Kaslov to justice."

"Even if it lands you in hot water at work?"

Preston stifled a regretful sigh. "Even if."

Chapter Four
Sabina

Sabina parked in her building's new allotted space and dragged herself up the stairs. The team had done a quick in-and-out that'd cost her a much-needed weekend off. Unlike the last mission, this one ended well, leaving the entire detachment pumped. But they'd been awake for almost forty-eight hours, and she was badly in need of some serious downtime.

She supposed she could get caught up on some this evening. She was young. A night or two of sleep and she'd bounce back.

She marveled at some of the older members of Bear's Brigade. Colonel Bustamante had let it slip he was forty-six. Lieutenant Colonel Johnson admitted to being almost that old, and she could tell from Major Watkins's almost totally salt-and-pepper hair and laugh lines he was somewhere in their ballpark. But the three not only kept up with the younger soldiers, they led them.

She wondered if the same was true of the older cops in the crowd tonight. Some of them were still trim and fit, but others had enjoyed a few too many Krispy Kremes.

She chided herself. Definitely bias.

The officers in her class hadn't been what she expected. She'd thought she'd be facing mostly old white men, but her students had been a cross-section. She laughed to herself. Despite having taught the course for three years now, it seemed she was every bit as biased as the next person.

Officer Ramos was Latino, although there was no trace of an accent in his voice. He sounded like any other rich boy from South Texas.

Boy, *her* inner bias really was showing this evening.

She was almost all the way up the stairs when a man moved out of the shadows. "Sabina?"

She stiffened until the voice registered. "Uncle Milo?"

So much for getting to bed at a reasonable hour. But an evening with her Uncle Milo waylaid sleep any time.

"In the flesh. I'm in town on business and thought I'd drop by and treat you to dinner somewhere." Her uncle flashed his trademark grin, the one that had gotten him into beds and out of scrapes most of his adult life. The grin she loved dearly but didn't quite trust.

The same grin Dominic wore when he was up to something.

But she loved her uncle and hadn't seen him in far too long. She wrapped her arms around him for a huge hug. "I would absolutely love to go out to dinner with you. If it's something simple so I don't have to get beautiful." She unlocked the door and ushered him inside.

"Simple works for me. And no worries. You're already beautiful." His grin morphed into a genuine smile.

She dumped the laptop and speaker and quickly changed into civvies. Milo suggested Mexican, and soon they were sitting in a back booth in her favorite taco joint. They gave their orders to the waiter and started on the basket of chips and salsa.

"Wonderful, absolutely wonderful. I don't know why they can't do Mexican this well in Houston," Milo groused.

"They do other stuff in Houston better than here." Sabina dipped a chip in the spicy salsa and popped it in her mouth. "What have you been up to these days? Mom was put out when you missed Christmas."

"Ah, well. I spent the holidays in the company of a beautiful young *señorita* down in Puerto Vallarta. I'd hoped I'd be bringing her home and introducing her to the family. But alas, she was only interested in a bit of a fling." Milo shrugged eloquently.

"Sounds like she figured you out," Sabina said dryly. "Let me guess. She isn't all that beautiful or that young, but she's loaded. Another rich widow, or was this one a pretty divorcée who scored a huge settlement?"

"Her late husband sold his part of a tech start-up a few years back. Regina will never have to work another day in her life. I was hoping she and I could become something special to each other."

Sabina sighed. "In other words, you wanted to marry her for her money. What would she have been? Number three?"

"Four. But I really love Regina."

"You've really loved all of them. I don't understand why you keep marrying these sugar mamas when you're making a good living as a pharmaceutical rep."

He looked at her ruefully. "I guess because I can. So how have things been with you?"

"Not wonderful." She cocked her head and looked at him. "Have you seen Dominic lately?"

"Had dinner with him last week. He's something else." Milo's eyes gleamed proudly. Milo had gone straight, but there was a part of him that admired the nephew who hadn't.

"One way to describe it. I'm curious. Did he mention anything he's been up to lately?"

"Like what?"

"Like any new, uh, schemes?"

"You mean, has he pulled any more fast ones? Sabina, if he's into something illegal, he's not going to tell anyone about it. Anyway, I thought they acquitted him."

"They did. This is something else."

"Like what?"

She thought a minute and chose her words carefully. "There are those here in San Antonio who believe he may have helped himself to money that's not his. The fallout landed directly in my lap and caused considerable trouble."

"For you?"

"For me and for his accuser. I'm hoping his accuser is wrong, but Dominic's been into some of this kind of stuff before."

Milo's eyes danced. "And may be again. He said he's onto something big that could have him sitting pretty for years. Wouldn't surprise me a bit. Wouldn't bother me all that much, either."

Sabina groaned inwardly. "Uncle Milo, the family's supposed to've gone straight. He has no business being 'onto something.'" She made air quotes with her fingers. "He damn near went to prison last year for 'something.'"

"Ah, well." He made a shooing motion with his hand. "He didn't, and he won't this time. You worry too much."

"It could have serious consequences for me. Sergeant. Army. Security clearance. Remember?"

Milo met and held her gaze. "You're also his sister. That should mean something to you."

"I am, and it does. But if push comes to shove, I'm not defending him at the expense of my career."

Milo changed the subject, and Sabina let him. The enchiladas were delicious, and she enjoyed her uncle, who was a delightful raconteur. But she couldn't shake her concern.

Of all the family, Milo was the *iffiest* in terms of staying straight, except for Dominic. Milo might not be running scams, but he seemed fine with whatever Dominic did. Clearly, he got a kick out of it. He didn't seem to have a clue how Dominic's behavior could ruin things for her and their family.

If Dominic had scammed the Ramos family and got caught and convicted, she'd bet the Army would have plenty to say to her about it. The job she loved could disappear in a heartbeat, and she'd be damned if she let that happen.

Her father needed to have a heart-to-heart with Dominic, and she was fine with instigating that happening right away.

It was almost twenty-three hundred, but her parents were night owls, and her father picked up on the first ring. "Did Milo find you?" he asked cheerfully.

"He did. We had a great plate of enchiladas. Has Mom forgiven him for missing Christmas?"

"Not yet. Maybe by April. So, I love you and you love me, but you never call this late for a chat unless something's going on. What's on your mind?"

"Dominic. There's some trouble he may be in."

Her father was silent for a minute. "What do you mean?"

"I mean all hell came down on my head a month ago because a business owner here in San Antonio thinks Dominic swindled ten million dollars from his company. His son's a cop, and he brought me to the station for questioning. It made me late for something important at work, and the consequences weren't good."

"I see. Is there any proof, or is it idle accusations?"

"I have no idea. But you know Dominic."

"True, I know my son. Did he talk to you about whatever's going on?"

"No. He talked to Uncle Milo. Who, of course, could care less. He kind of admires Dominic, if you want to know the truth. Dad, you need to talk to him. Tell him to cut it out, whatever he's doing."

"I have absolutely no influence with your brother, and you know it."

"You might if you told him what it could do to the family, and if you stopped turning a blind eye. You know as well as I do he was guilty of swindling that old couple, and he damn near went to prison for it. One of these days his luck's gonna run out. He's not made of Teflon.

"Unless someone in this family says something that persuades him to stop, he's going to wind up in prison. As pissed as that family is, it could very well be now."

Her father was silent for a moment. "Why do you care? It's Dominic's life and his business if he chooses to skirt the law. It's not my concern, and frankly, it's not yours either. I'm tired of worrying about him. Your mother and I are getting old and shouldn't have to waste what time we have left worrying about a grown man who we have no control over."

"Dad, I'm sorry he's caused you so much worry. But at the same time, if that's the family's attitude, it's no wonder people like the cop and his family think poorly of us. And why wouldn't my brother's behavior be my concern? He's a reflection on *me*. I'm a Kaslov too. He pulls some shit and gets into trouble, it's my security clearance at risk. Do you really think it's fair for him to wreck my career because he'd rather steal than work for a living?"

"He's also your brother," her father snapped. "Doesn't that mean anything to you?"

"Of course it does. But, do you ask him the same question when it seems he could care less what shit he brings down on my head? I've worked long and hard to have a military career I'm proud of, and I'll be damned if I let his criminal behavior ruin it."

"If that's the way you feel," he said tightly.

"Damn it, Dad. I was detained by the cop for so long, three people *died* because I wasn't there to help them. It isn't only me who gets screwed over by Dominic."

She heard her father's sharp intake of breath. "All right. I'll talk to him. For all the good it will do."

"Thank you, Dad. Have a good night."

Damn. She hadn't meant to argue with her father, and she was sorry Dominic had given their parents so much to worry about. But she meant every word she said. Dominic was not going to wreck her career.

Sabina rolled her neck and was about to head to the refrigerator for a carton of ice cream when Colonel Bustamante's ringtone sang out. She grabbed her phone. "Kaslov." She listened for a moment, and a huge smile bloomed on her face. "Yes, sir. I understand. An hour and a half. See you."

Ice cream forgotten, she changed into a clean uniform, grabbed her freshly packed go bag, her tool and weapons duffle, and headed for the car, nearly forgetting to lock her front door in her excitement.

Her fingers were sweating, and she tasted the anticipation at the prospect of another mission. She'd find out more about it on the small charter plane used to ferry whatever group of soldiers had been chosen for the assignment to wherever they were needed.

Her earlier fatigue forgotten, she went over the speed limit and took the expressway entrance ramp to head to a small private airfield outside town where their plane would be waiting.

She lived for these assignments. She was doing something meaningful with her life and having a great time doing it.

Dominic wasn't going to fuck it up for her.

Chapter Five

Preston

Preston trudged into the meeting room and sank down onto the hard chair, wishing to hell he didn't have this asinine class tonight and could spend the evening in his recliner with a fistful of ibuprofen and a beer chaser. He'd gotten roughed up breaking up a brawl in a grocery store parking lot, triggered by an argument over a handicapped parking space. His arms were scraped up despite his long-sleeved shirt, and his right knee was skinned and swollen. He stretched out his legs in front of him and wondered for the hundredth time if the sergeant was going to show tonight.

She'd missed the last two classes, and he was beginning to wonder if she'd any intention of finishing the course. For some perverse reason, he found it irritating. He hadn't wanted to take the class in the first place and had no reason to be pissed because she was a no-show. He didn't understand why he gave a damn.

Okay. He knew why and had no intention of going down that road, so he had to cut that shit out before he did something more stupid than he'd already done.

He was pissed at her lack of consideration. The second week the class had all shown up as requested, and somebody he didn't know had finally reached the base, only to learn the sergeant was away on a "training mission."

The base had contacted the PD the following week, and they'd all gotten an email the day before the class was scheduled to meet. He'd heard nothing until seventeen hundred when a tersely worded message informed him the class was meeting and his presence was required. He shook his head. If this was the way the Army did things, it was a wonder they ever won a war.

The disgruntled cops drifted in one by one. At the stroke of nineteen hundred, the sergeant limped into the room, carrying the laptop and speaker.

Damn. She was in worse shape than he was.

She had a bruise on her face that was going from purple to green. Her arms were covered with scratches, she sported a number of bug bites, and she had a sunburn that was darkening into a deep tan. "Jesus, what happened to you?" he blurted before he could stop himself.

"I was in the field. Training maneuvers," she said dismissively.

Yeah, sure. He'd been in the Army. He'd been on training maneuvers, and none of them left soldiers in the shape she was in this evening.

He was more curious about her than ever. Which was such a bad idea on so many levels. He knew better yet leaned into the curiosity.

The rest of the class wandered in while she set up her equipment. She had the decency to apologize for her absences as she looked around at the class.

"Our last training session addressed recognizing and confronting overt bias," she said. "This evening we're going to look at covert bias. This is much harder to confront because it's insidious. Frequently we don't recognize it in ourselves or see it in others. In fact, most of us pride ourselves on not having biases we actually have."

The next hour was surprisingly interesting. She passed out a questionnaire with various scenarios listed and asked how the described situation would make them feel. Situations like seeing two men holding hands, or walking by a mentally disabled person talking loudly in the grocery store, or there's a twenty-year age difference between lab partners.

They were given a few minutes to answer, and then the sergeant instructed them in the grading process. Her eyes danced as she looked around the room. "Anybody learn anything new about themselves?"

"I must have a real thing about fat people," one of the women said. "I never realized."

"Now that you know it, do you think it will affect your treatment of our overweight citizens?"

"I don't know. I thought I was nice to them."

"You came down like a brick on your daughter-in-law when she gained a bunch of baby weight," the other woman reminded her.

"Huh. I don't even remember doing it."

Some of the others volunteered their results.

A couple of the younger officers admitted to having bias against the elderly and disabled. One of the older cops said he'd scored low on sexuality but high on gender, which he didn't understand.

Preston looked down at his scores. Nothing really jumped out. Even the questions on race reflected mild to moderate negative feelings. But those were questions about race in general, not specifically about any one group. He substituted gypsy anywhere there was a race moniker and answered the questions again.

The score was markedly different. He wasn't surprised. There was nothing unconscious about his bias against the Romani.

She spent the rest of the evening leading the class in a discussion of identifying and dealing with unconscious prejudice. His phone vibrated in his pocket twice, but he made it a practice not to check it when he was otherwise occupied.

As soon as class was over, he stepped into the hall and looked at his phone. His mother had texted him three times.

Emergency. Call home immediately.

Well, hell. His mother wasn't a dire circumstances person. Something serious must be going on. Preston's blood ran cold. His folks seemed okay when he saw them for dinner on Sunday, but the axe could fall swiftly and hard at their age.

He called, and his mother answered on the first ring. "Your brother's disappeared."

"Jeremy? Disappeared? Mom, what are you talking about?"

"Nobody's seen him for a week. He was supposed to be at work, but his new administrative aide said he's not shown up since last Wednesday. I went by his apartment, and it looks like nobody's been there for a while, either."

"Has he called? Texted? Sent anybody an email?"

"Your father got a text this morning. It says something about leaving and no choice."

"Which tells me nothing. Please go get Dad's phone and read it to me?"

He heard her walking through the condo. She demanded his father's phone and came back on a moment later. "It reads 'Leaving country. Have to do this. No choice. Money.' It's like he didn't have a chance to finish what he was sending."

"Leaving country, have to do this, no choice, money? What's that supposed to mean?"

"We don't know. That's why we called you. Do you think it could have something to do with that Dominic person who took our money?"

"I don't know, Mom." But he knew somebody who might.

He'd have to talk to her again. He would do it carefully this time. He sure as fuck didn't want any more trouble falling on his head. "What does Dad want me to do?"

"Do you know any of the PIs around town? Your dad wants to hire someone to find Jeremy. Someone who isn't bound by the rules and ethics of the legal system like you are."

"I know several. I'll reach out to them tomorrow."

"Thank you."

"I'd tell you not to worry, but I know you will anyway. I'll get back to you by noon tomorrow."

He jogged to the parking lot. He needed to talk to Sergeant Kaslov before she left.

He didn't plan on getting in trouble again, but he would at least ask her what she knew.

She was putting the laptop and speaker in her trunk when he walked up. She turned and stiffened when she noted the expression on his face.

"Can I help you?" She'd dropped her engaging instructor voice and looked at him coldly.

"My brother's disappeared. Do you know anything about it?"

She looked at him with exasperation. "You never learn, do you? No, I don't know where your brother is. Since you're out here giving me the third degree, I'm guessing you think my brother has something to do with it, and somehow I'm supposed to know what."

"It crossed my mind."

"The answer is no. I have no idea what Dominic's up to, and I doubt he knows where your brother is or what he's doing. Haven't you learned anything sitting there on your ass in my class?"

"I've learned a lot, none of which has any bearing on this situation. My brother's disappeared after sending a cryptic message saying it involves money and he had no choice in the matter. It's a reasonable assumption to believe your brother might have something to do with, I don't know, maybe taking the money because he was in on it."

She stiffened. "What did the message say?"

He hesitated. But what the hell. "'Leaving country. Have to do this. No choice. Money.' We don't think he went voluntarily. He's got an important position in the company, not one he can simply walk away from and not be missed." Okay. That was a bit of a lie, but she wouldn't know that. "We're concerned enough to hire a private detective to look into it."

"I see. Look. I get that you're worried. If it were my brother, I would be too. But I don't know anything, and I doubt my brother does either. Would you excuse me?" She slammed the trunk shut and got in her car, then started the engine and drove away with a slight tire screech.

Preston scowled at her retreating vehicle, got into his truck, and peeled out of the parking lot a little faster than he should've.

Damn it. He wanted to push her, but if her heels were dug in, she wasn't going to tell him anything, and he'd get in more trouble if he kept pushing. Maybe the PI could find out what was going on. He sure as hell hoped so.

Jeremy was an idiot, but he was Preston's idiot, and Preston loved his little brother with all his heart.

Which made him think beyond his anger.

Sergeant Kaslov probably loved her brother too and was willing to lie to protect him. The entire Kaslov family probably felt the same. Which left him SOL.

He hoped to hell the PI would find Jeremy, because if Preston waited for Sergeant Kaslov to tell him anything, he'd be in the dark forever.

***

Sabina

Sabina finished off the last of the garlic shrimp and macaroni salad she'd picked up at the Hawaiian fast-food place down from her apartment complex. She'd started to call her father and her uncle, but she'd missed lunch and was starving. Besides, if she was going to have words with her father again, she wanted to do it on a full stomach.

She hadn't talked to her parents since the night she and her father quarreled. She'd been gone for weeks, and even if she'd been home, she doubted she would've spoken with him. Her father was the kind of man who needed time to stew before he came around. He'd probably be stewing again after tonight's call. She didn't relish tangling with him again, but if Dominic had something to do with Jeremy Ramos's disappearance, she needed to know.

Her father answered on the third ring. "Where have you been? Your mother's been concerned."

"Same place I always am. Another training mission. I left right after we talked and didn't get back until yesterday." She knew damn well her parents suspected she was more than an instructor. But they'd never mentioned it, and she couldn't.

"I see. Okay, then. I can tell your mom at least one of her chickadees is back where they belong."

The hair stood up on her arms. "Dominic isn't?"

"No, and your mother's worried. We haven't talked to him since before you and I talked the last time."

"So you didn't have a chance to ask him what was going on?"

"No, I didn't. It wasn't for lack of trying. Your mother and I have tried to reach him at least every other day for the last week or so. After we got the text."

"You got a text from him?"

"He sent us this odd message. He was going to be gone for a while and not to worry about him. Said he would send his mother an alpaca sweater or a silver bracelet."

Alpaca sweater. Silver bracelet. Those were souvenirs from a few countries in South America.

"Did he say he was alone, or was he with someone? Jeremy perhaps?"

"Sabina, you know as much as I do. I wish we knew where he was."

"If he's out of the country, he might not have an international phone plan." She bit her lip. Her father didn't know anything. Asking if Dominic was with Jeremy was pointless. If Dominic was up to his old tricks, pointing out the possibility to her father wasn't going to accomplish anything but worry her parents. "Thanks for the information."

"Such as it was. So will you be in town for a while or off on another training mission?"

"I never know, Dad."

They exchanged a few more pleasantries and said good night.

She looked up Uncle Milo's number and punched it in. It was about to go to voicemail when her uncle answered, breathless.

"What can I do for you, Sabina?" She heard a woman's voice and the rustling of sheets.

Oops. It was a wonder he'd answered at all.

"I'm calling about Dominic. Have you talked to him since you saw me in San Antonio?"

"No. Why? Is something going on?"

"It may be."

"Give me a minute." She heard him mumble something that sounded like, "Hand me my robe," then he came back on after a brief pause.

"I'm sorry if I disturbed your evening," Sabina said, glad they weren't on FaceTime.

"It's all good. Now, what about Dominic?"

"You remember when we talked, I said a family here in San Antonio's accusing him of swindling their son and the family company out of a lot of money? Well, that same son has disappeared after sending a text saying he had to leave the country, he had no choice, and it involved money.

"I just talked to Dad, and Dominic sent a message to them saying he was going to be gone a while and would send Mom an alpaca sweater or a silver bracelet, which sounds like he's somewhere in South America. When he talked to you, exactly what did he say?"

She heard Milo's sudden intake of breath. "Emeralds. He said something about emeralds."

Colombia.

"What specifically did he say about them?"

Uncle Milo didn't say anything for a long moment. "Nothing specific. Just that there was money, lots of money in emeralds, especially if you knew somebody official."

"Somebody official? Anything else?"

"No. That's pretty much it. Why? Do you think he and the other guy are down there?"

"I have no idea. But his family's concerned, and so are Mom and Dad."

"They can worry all they want. It's not changing anything. Sabina, your brother's gonna do what he's gonna do, and none of you have any control over him. The other man's probably the same. Y'all need to go on about your lives. Dominic will be home when he's home. So will the other guy. Now, can I get back to my lovely lady before she gets fed up and puts on her clothes and leaves?"

Sabina giggled. "By all means. And thanks for the information."

Which she would keep to herself. Her mother and father didn't need more to worry about, and she wasn't about to tell Preston Ramos or his family anything.

She threw the takeout carton in the trash and treated herself to a long, hot shower and a glass of wine while she mulled over what she'd learned.

The information from her uncle about emeralds and officials were two big pieces of a vague puzzle. Perhaps Dominic thought he had an in with some corrupt government officials. There had been chatter lately referencing unscrupulous South American officials, particularly in Colombia.

Well, shit. She hoped her brother hadn't gotten involved in the corrupt emerald trade, but she wouldn't put it past him. And she wouldn't be surprised if he'd managed to suck Jeremy Ramos into one of his harebrained schemes.

The question was what to do about it, if anything. She thought briefly of sharing what she'd learned with the cop and promptly dismissed it. He and his father would jump to the conclusion that Dominic was at fault and that Jeremy was again the victim of her brother's machinations. While she didn't think that was a big mental leap when it came to Dominic, she had no idea what was going on. But until she knew more, she wasn't sharing anything with anyone.

Actually, there was one person she could talk to. With Dominic's reference to officials, it might be something her boss would want to look into.

Corrupt Colombian officials had come up on a mission a few months ago, and since then the colonel had mentioned he'd been kept apprised of the mostly inconsequential chatter. She had no idea if the situation with Dominic and Jeremy would be of any interest or importance, but she could run it by Colonel Bustamante and let him decide what, if anything, they could do about it.

***

Sabina looked up to see it was almost quitting time before she and the colonel could shake loose. She stepped into his office and offered a quick salute to Lieutenant Highsmith, who was staffing the office with her usual aplomb.

"He's waiting for you," the lieutenant said with a warm smile.

Colonel Bustamante was seated behind his desk, sipping a late afternoon coffee from his favorite oversized mug with "Bear's Brigade" written across both sides. He looked up with his usual professional smile, and Sabina gave him a quick salute. "What can I do for you, Sergeant?"

She returned his smile and sat across from him without being invited. Behind closed doors and on missions, Bear's soldiers were much less formal than when they were in front of other Army personnel. The brass didn't seem to hold the informality against them, especially with their success rate.

"I've become aware of something I'm concerned about. I want to run it by you and see what you think."

He nodded and folded his hands in front of him. "Fire away."

She started with the most recent "discussion" with Preston, and then outlined the conversations with her father and uncle.

"So both young men have disappeared after leaving similar messages with their families," the colonel said. "The Ramos boy implied he was going along against his will. Your brother hinted he was going to South America and said something about emeralds and officials. Interesting. Especially considering the chatter coming out of South America."

"The bit about emeralds and officials is what worries me," Sabina said. "He said it to Uncle Milo, who doesn't have a problem with the stuff Dominic does. Which makes me think whatever he's up to isn't harmless."

"Does Ramos think his brother's up to something?"

"He thinks Dominic had something to do with the disappearance. The family's hiring a PI to find him."

"Which he may not be able to do if he's out of the country." He paused before saying, "It's worth looking into, which I'll do, but most likely, it's nothing to worry about."

She breathed a sigh of relief. "Thank you, Colonel. I appreciate it."

That was a weight off her shoulders.

If Colonel Bustamante didn't think there was anything to worry about, there probably wasn't.

With her shoulders less tense, she headed toward the mall for a little retail therapy and pizza at the food court.

Chapter Six
Sabina

Sabina looked around at the roomful of youthful faces in front of her, ready for combat medic training. She'd had this group for several weeks now, minus the time she was in Brazil on the latest mission, during which Sergeant Wang, her usual substitute, was in charge. He'd spoken highly of them, and after a couple of classes and an exam they'd aced, she could see why.

"Today we're going to start the portion of the course dealing with treating soldiers exposed to weapons of mass destruction: chemical, biological, radiological, and nuclear. Despite the well-deserved fear and horror these weapons generate in the hearts and minds of all of us, there's a tremendous amount we can do to treat a soldier exposed to one of these weapons."

Her phone vibrated in her pocket. She'd let it be known far and wide she didn't answer the phone during class, so it was nearly an hour before she pulled it out and checked it for texts. There was only one, a terse message from the colonel.

Meeting at 1600 re Thurs discussion.

Interesting. It'd been nearly a week since she'd gone to Colonel Bustamante with her concerns, and when no more was said, she'd assumed that was the end of it.

Apparently not.

The meeting was in less than an hour, so she spent a few minutes in her tiny office grading the latest exams before heading to the colonel's office. Her curiosity was piqued: she didn't know if she should be concerned. Best case scenario would be he hadn't found anything.

Her hopes were dashed when Lieutenant Highsmith directed her down the hall to the general's office. "Colonel Bustamante and General McKinley are waiting for you in the general's office."

Her heart sank.

Dominic, what have you gotten yourself into?

General McKinley's new administrative aide, a no-nonsense lieutenant with her glasses perched on her nose, motioned Sabina to the office. Her mouth dry, she stepped in and saluted both senior officers. Colonel Bustamante motioned her to the remaining chair.

"Thank you for bringing your brother's situation to our attention," General McKinley said solemnly.

"Of course, sir." She looked from one man to the other.

"Sergeant Kaslov, we've located both your brother and Jeremy Ramos in Cartagena," Colonel Bustamante said. "They flew down together two and a half weeks ago on a commercial flight under their real names. We can't determine if Jeremy's there because he was coerced. However, it appears he's there willingly."

Sabina took in a deep breath. *Huh. I bet the Ramos family would never believe that.*

The colonel continued. "It wouldn't be any business of the government, but since their arrival, rumors have been flying about two *norteamericanos* reaching out to a mysterious high-level government official in hopes of doing some illegal emerald trading.

"There have been rumors to this effect for years, that someone high up in the government is corrupt and has, among other things, dealt in the illegal emerald trade. He's rumored to be ruthless, including ordering the murders of his competition and anyone in the government who's tried to ascertain his identity.

"It's been years, and still no one knows who this individual is. Our government is concerned because the chatter is some of the money this official is making is being funneled to terrorist groups operating from Central America, all the way north into our southern states. The descriptions of the two Americans reaching out to this man match those of your brother and Jeremy Ramos."

Well, shit. "Do you have pictures of Dominic and Jeremy?"

"We do. Driver's licenses and passports. It's interesting that they traveled under their own names and IDs," the colonel said.

"It doesn't surprise me. Dominic is that naïve and that arrogant," Sabina stated. "Or he's innocent."

"But you don't believe that," the general prompted.

"I would have a hard time believing it, sir. It's the emeralds comment he made to our uncle, about there being money in them, especially if you knew someone official."

Both men nodded. "He couldn't have come out and said it much plainer," the colonel said.

"Both our government and Colombia's would like to learn the identity of this official," the general shared.

As she nodded, the men looked at one another.

"It needs to be checked out," the general said gruffly. "Two American citizens seeking to communicate with this particular Colombian official about illegal emeralds has grave implications. For years, the Colombian government has been trying to determine the identity of this corrupt official, as have we. This might be our opportunity to find out who it is."

Sabina's head whirled. Using her brother's illegal activity, the U.S. government would aid the Colombian government in bringing down a corrupt official in their country.

Dominic had graduated from petty theft and graft to a crime that could become an international incident, with a side helping of a black ops mission.

He was going to be in so much trouble, he'd never get out of it.

Way to go, you selfish asshole.

He should've stuck to swindling old people.

The colonel turned to Sabina. "I foresee needing your skill set on the mission and have spoken about the potential conflict of interest with"—he tilted his head in the general's direction—"my superior officers. We are of the mind that you will be able to handle the mission in the manner to which we are accustomed. Professionally. Do you believe you can objectively participate in a mission where your brother may be culpable, or is this cutting too close to the bone?"

"I'm able to carry out the mission, sir." She thought of the conversation she'd had with her father. Talk about prophetic.

"We'll put a plan together and go wheels up the day after tomorrow," the colonel said.

"Sir, do we involve the Ramos family in this?" she asked.

"No. Why would we?" The colonel looked puzzled.

"Officer Ramos said they intended to hire a PI to look for Dominic and Jeremy. They have the money to do it. A good PI would probably have located them by now. If he gets to them first, things could go sideways fast. We might lose Dominic and Jeremy."

"We can't have a civilian interloper anywhere near this," General McKinley said. "Colonel, Sergeant, the two of you need to pay the senior Mr. Ramos a visit. Tell him to call off his PI and let the government take care of this mess."

"If he refuses?"

"Tell him we're prepared to do whatever it takes to carry out this mission successfully." He gave her a baleful glare. "Whatever."

The colonel nodded. "Got it."

Sabina blinked. She'd seen "whatever" a few times, and it was never pretty.

She saluted the general, and she and Colonel Bustamante left the general's office.

"Best to get this over with quickly," the colonel advised.

"Yes, sir."

She wondered if the phrase "the apple doesn't fall far from the tree" applied to the elder Ramos. If so, he'd be the giant asshole who set the example for his sons.

***

Preston

Preston left the substation and trudged to his truck. He'd gotten another roughing up yesterday, breaking up a brawl in front of an inner-city middle school triggered by a long-standing gang rivalry. At least the young gang bangers had chosen to limit themselves to brass knuckles and fists instead of the knives and guns used by the older gang members at the high school down the way.

His head had ached unmercifully during class last night, and he honestly couldn't remember a thing about whatever Sergeant Kaslov had covered. Thankfully, it'd been the last week of that crap, and he and his fellow sinners were done. Not that she hadn't made some good points. If he'd been there under other circumstances, he probably would've appreciated the insights and tools offered. But he was still torqued about being suspended and still held loads of reservations about Sabina Kaslov.

And was irritated as hell that he couldn't stop thinking about fucking her brains out.

He was almost to the truck when his phone rang. He looked down and saw the call was from his dad, who never called during the workday unless it was an emergency.

Since they were all waiting on pins and needles to hear from Jeremy, he hollered, "Dad?"

"I need you to come straight to my office, even if you have to leave before your shift's over."

Arrogant asshole. "I'm already off. What is it? Have you heard from Jeremy?"

"Just come. I'll explain when you get here."

Preston stared at the phone. Wow. He hadn't heard that tone of voice out of his father in years. The shit must have hit the fan, big-time.

He headed downtown and parked under the building of the company's offices. The elevator took him to the top floor, where Agnes, his father's long-time secretary, waved him in. His mouth dropped open, and he stared at Sergeant Kaslov and her imposing commanding officer, Colonel Benevides. Benacio. No. Bustamante.

Preston's lips tightened. He didn't know if they'd come to complain again. If they had, they weren't going to find anywhere near as sympathetic an audience as they had from the SAPD.

The sergeant and the colonel both nodded. His father motioned to the last empty chair in the room and turned to the colonel. "Tell him what you just told me."

Colonel Bustamante leaned forward in his chair. His face was cool, professional, and devoid of emotion, giving no clue as to why his news had impacted Preston's father so strongly.

"This is regarding your questions made to Sergeant Kaslov last week about her knowledge of your brother's whereabouts. She asked me to look into it, and we did. In short, the government's determined your brother and Dominic Kaslov flew to Colombia two and a half weeks ago.

"Since then we've received intel that two *norteamericanos* matching their descriptions have been reaching out to known operators involved in emerald smuggling, including a Colombian official long suspected of being part of the corrupt emerald trade.

"Neither our government nor the Colombians know the identity of this individual and feel this is an excellent opportunity to learn exactly who this person is. The scope of the opportunity will be the observation and apprehension of the official, as well as the likely apprehension of the Americans involved.

"This operation will be carried out by a detachment of the Army under the auspices of the State Department. We're telling you this as a courtesy, as we understand you have a PI employed to find Ramos and Kaslov. You need to call off your PI and let the government handle it."

Preston stared at the colonel. "You mean to tell me you and the sergeant have the unmitigated gall to walk in here, inform us you intend to arrest an innocent man who's been forced to go out of the country against his will, and expect us to do your bidding? I'm sure my father has already refused. Let me add my refusal to his. If anything, it's more imperative than ever for our PI to find Jeremy and rescue him before something even more serious happens to him."

The colonel raised his eyebrow. "The State Department has determined this is a matter of national security. In case you missed it, we're not asking you to recall your PI, we're telling you. Otherwise, there will be consequences."

Preston stared at the colonel in shock. He was certain Bustamante had just threatened to "remove" the PI if he interfered with a government operation. Preston glanced over at his father, who looked as stunned as he felt.

His father recovered first. "This situation is entirely unfair to my son, who's already down there against his will."

"We have found differently, Mr. Ramos," the colonel said grimly. "Neither of them are there against their will. They took a commercial flight and traveled under their own names. If your son had been coerced, the other party would've had false ID made to conceal his identity."

"It appears you're prepared to let this scenario play out and eliminate any chance of his rescue. Does the welfare of an American citizen mean nothing to our government?" Preston's father asked loftily.

Bustamante and the sergeant exchanged glances. "We're not going to discuss our mission and tactics with you. Suffice it to say, we will take every precaution to ensure the safety of our citizens."

"We're. We. Our." Preston looked at Sabina as the pieces swiftly fell into place. The absences. The shape she was in when she returned to class all banged up. The tools and weapons she had with her the night he apprehended her. The dire consequences of the detainment that had so infuriated the Army brass.

Sabina was part of a black ops team, likely headed up by Colonel Bustamante. Her primary job, with being a training instructor as a convenient cover.

A woman in black ops. Who would believe it?

"Seems to me," Preston ground out, "that your mission supersedes lives. My brother's life, to be exact."

The colonel turned a laser stare on Preston's father. "This is a government operation. As such, no interference will be tolerated. We're not out to harm or kill your son, but the bottom line is that national security comes first. We will carry out our mission. Period."

The colonel nodded to Sabina, and they both stood. They were almost to the door when Preston's father called out, "Wait, please. We need to talk about this some more."

"Actually, we don't," the colonel said.

"Yes, yes we do." Preston's father dropped his bravado and looked like a man on the edge. "Please. I want to talk to you as a parent who loves his child. Please listen to me for a minute before you walk out of here." He looked at the colonel. "I'm asking as a father."

The colonel stopped so swiftly, Sabina almost ran into him. He turned and sat down. "Five minutes."

Sabina sat looking baffled.

Preston's father looked from Colonel Bustamante to Sabina. "You need to take Preston with you on your mission."

Preston forced himself not to react. His father had to be out of his mind if he thought Preston was going on a fool's errand with an Army black ops team.

Sabina looked over at his father, disbelief coating her expression.

The colonel shook his head. "That's out of the question." He started to stand.

"Why is it out of the question?" Preston's father demanded. "You're going to need Preston."

Sabina winced.

"What's so unbelievable about that?" Preston snapped.

"Sorry," she said. "I don't mean…" She gestured at nothing in particular.

"What the sergeant is too polite to say is, the suggestion is ludicrous," Colonel Bustamante said baldly. "There's no way we'd take Officer Ramos. It's out of the question."

Preston bristled. "I was an Army Ranger, and now I'm a cop. I'd fit in. I'm trained in tactics you probably employ, and I use my Army training in my police work. I would be an asset if for no other reason than I know my brother better than you do."

"You're also pushing forty and have been out of the military for years. I promise you SAPD's fitness requirements aren't stringent compared to the fitness level we maintain," Sabina said dryly.

He ground his teeth. Like Bustamante wasn't older than him.

His father interjected, "As Preston said, he knows his brother better than you do. It pains me to say this, but Jeremy may be down there of his own free will. He's headstrong, impulsive, and sometimes isn't the savviest individual. It's quite possible he's fallen under the influence of this woman's brother and is choosing to do the things he's being accused of. He's also distrustful of authority figures and likely to do the opposite of what someone such as yourself orders him to do. He would listen to his brother."

Which was utter bullshit. Jeremy wouldn't listen to him any more than he would anyone else. His father was up to something, and he had a feeling he knew what.

"Why?" Sabina asked. "His brother's an authority figure."

"He's also my brother," Preston improvised. "The one I read stories to and cuddled when he had a nightmare. Dad's right. He would listen to me when he wouldn't listen to anybody else."

"You do realize you could get yourself killed down there," Sabina said. She turned to his father. "Are you willing to risk sacrificing one son to save the other?"

His father's face froze. "It will be your job to see that doesn't happen."

"Which is exactly why we *won't* be taking him," the colonel said firmly.

"Colonel Bustamante, I know it's not the way the Army usually works, but you need to make an exception. By not taking him, you're condemning your mission to failure. I know for a fact Jeremy isn't going to listen to a thing your soldiers have to say," Roel said solemnly. "If this mission is as crucial as you say, take Preston. He's your only chance of success."

"Even if it puts Preston's life in danger?" Sabina asked.

They sat in a pool of tense silence. His father turned to him. "Preston, I know it's risky, but I still need you to go. Are you willing to join them if they'll take you?"

"Yeah." Not that he wanted to. It was the last thing he wanted to do. To go on a fool's errand to find his brother in South America. But his father had something up his sleeve, some reason he wanted Preston along. Probably to see that nothing happened to Jeremy since their father needed Jeremy to run the company. Which, after this clusterfuck, made no sense at all.

Per usual, his father expected Preston to fall in line and do what was asked.

He sighed inwardly. Yet again doing his father's bidding, but this time he didn't have much choice. He loved his brother, and the family would be devastated if he died. So Preston would go because the detachment the colonel was sending sure as hell wasn't going to make sure his brother didn't come home in a body bag.

The colonel turned to face him. "Convince me to take you."

"I'll do my best with my brother to get him to do what you need him to do."

"I'm not convinced."

He looked at the colonel. "What do you want to hear?"

"Think a minute, Ranger. You'll figure it out."

Ah. "I'll follow orders. I'll do what I'm told."

"You're damned right you will. You'll follow orders to the letter. You'll do exactly what you're told, and you will *not* do one thing more than what you're told. You'll synthesize you're along for one reason and one reason only: to secure your brother's cooperation. *Not* to look after his best interests. Do you understand?"

Hardass.

Preston nodded.

"Sir, permission to speak freely," Sabina said.

"Go ahead, Sergeant."

"After the stunt he pulled with me last month, can we trust him? He has unresolved issues that'll put us in danger, the same way he caused the dire consequences we suffered the night he unlawfully detained me."

"Sergeant, with all due respect, I'm tired of hearing about dire consequences associated with your detention that evening," Preston snapped. "The Army has already expressed its outrage, and I've paid the price, literally, with a month's pay."

"The sergeant isn't exaggerating," the colonel said. "It was a shitshow. That's all you need to know. Now, are you going to drop your holier-than-thou attitude and follow any and all orders to the letter, or do we go wheels up without you?"

Ouch. He wasn't forgiven for whatever happened that night. Might not ever be.

"Colonel," his father broke in, "what we probably ought to be asking is if the sergeant is going to be part of this mission. You've stressed my son will not be there to look after his brother's best interests. Have you stressed the same to her?"

The colonel's lips thinned. "Mr. Ramos, we have afforded you more than all the courtesy you deserved. There's nothing else to discuss." He turned to face Preston and winged up a brow.

"Colonel, I'm prepared to follow orders to the letter. My personal feelings will not get in the way of your mission objective."

"We'll contact you tomorrow," the colonel said.

Preston's father put up his hand and said, "What if Jeremey needs the services of an attorney?"

"The government will provide one with the appropriate security clearance."

"Fine," his father snapped as if he was doing the colonel a favor.

The colonel and Sabina walked out the door and never looked back.

***

"Everything's been squared with the SAPD. We go wheels up tomorrow at zero six hundred. The sergeant will pick you up and drive you to an undisclosed location where we'll board a plane for Cartagena. You'll be issued DCUs that match what my soldiers wear. Additionally, bring some holiday-type clothing. The kind of stuff you'd wear as an American tourist. You and the sergeant will be an adventurous couple on vacation."

After being summoned at lunch, Preston was standing at parade rest next to Sabina, both of them in Colonel Bustamante's office getting the rundown on his deployment—there was a term he never thought would apply to him again—to South America.

"I see." *Well, shit.* The last thing he wanted to do was pretend to be part of a couple with Sabina. Yeah, he wanted to fuck her brains out, but he disliked and distrusted her. One had nothing to do with the other.

He glanced in her direction. She didn't look any happier about the assignment than he was.

She eyed him coolly. "How good an actor are you?"

He regarded her with equal detachment. "I guess we'll find out. You?"

She gave a half shrug. "I go undercover often. I've gotten good at it." In other words, he'd better be damned good. "I'll need your address," she reminded him.

She handed him her phone, and he punched in his address. She took it back and held it up. "Look at me." She snapped his photo and showed it to the colonel. "Will this work?"

"Good enough. They can clean it up." Colonel Bustamante turned to him. "The sergeant will pick you up tomorrow before zero five hundred. Leave your cell, wallet, and any jewelry you wear at your house. You have any tats?"

Preston nodded. "An Army Rangers tat, upper left arm."

"General or specific?"

Preston unbuttoned his SAPD uniform top and showed the colonel his tattoo.

"Good. General. Nice work."

As he rebuttoned his shirt, the colonel said, "Don't bring *anything* that could identify you as Preston Ramos. We'll have a new identity with the accompanying documentation in a wallet for you. You and Sabina can work up a cover story on the trip down."

"Cover story?"

"How we met, where we live, what we do," she said. "I'll walk you through it."

"A reminder, Ramos. We're breaking every rule letting you come with us," the colonel told him. "Do *not* make us regret it."

Chapter Seven
Sabina

Sabina pulled up in front of a small Craftsman-style house in the Deco District. It wasn't even zero five hundred, but it was pitch dark, and a late norther was spitting cold rain on the windshield. The front porch light was on, and there was shadowed movement through the living room sheers. She was about to get out of the car when the living room light went off, and the front door opened. Preston shut it behind him, turned to lock up, then walked to the car, where he tossed his duffle in the back seat and climbed in beside her, filling the passenger side of the car completely.

"It's a hot car, but there sure isn't much room in here."

She lifted her chin toward his driveway. "You could hold a dance in the front seat of your truck." She gestured to the cupholder on the console, with two white cups that had Folklores Coffee House brown sleeves around them. "The one on the right's yours. Stuff to doctor it with is in the little bag."

He lifted his cup and inhaled. "Wonderful. 'Preciate it."

"Sure."

They fell silent as she made her way out of the old neighborhood and onto an artery leading them out of town. She was a little surprised a man with Ramos money behind him would live in a small house in an older section of town, even if it was in one of the historic neighborhoods. Maybe his father didn't share, or cut him off for becoming a cop, or Preston chose to live on his cop salary so he wasn't beholden to his father, who was a real piece of work.

If he did live on his cop salary, the suspension without pay had to've hurt him, at least some.

Regardless, it wouldn't bring Kieran Lavigne back.

Traffic was light this early in the morning. As she made her way out of town, the windshield wipers slapped the wet away temporarily as she drove west on a farm-to-market road.

"You're a member of a black ops team," he said as she turned off onto a second road.

"I guess you could use that term. The Army doesn't call us that."

"What does the Army call you?"

"Nothing. We don't exist. We're instructors. Even Colonel Bustamante. The only reason you know about us is so we wouldn't't've to remove your private investigator. I trust you called him off."

"I finally reached him last night. He hadn't made any progress past the flights to Colombia and a Cartagena hotel. He hasn't spotted them since. The asshole didn't accomplish jack shit and still expects to be paid for his time."

"I should hope so." She took another turn.

"I'm surprised you didn't blindfold me or something, as hush-hush as y'all are."

"We use a different plane, pilot, and airstrip every time."

Preston huffed under his breath.

The clouds were barely beginning to lighten in the east when she spotted the rundown-looking gate leading into a pasture, the gravel drive barely visible for the rain puddles. She slammed the car in park and was about to get out when Preston beat her to it. "I'll get it."

He unlatched the gate and pulled it wide. She drove through, and he pushed it shut and got back in the car. "Are you sure you have the right place?"

"I'm sure."

He said nothing more as they bounced across a good two miles of potholed gravel and mud until they got to the small, abandoned airstrip where an older model Gulfstream waited.

She recognized fellow operative Sergeant Jazz Washington's Jeep and Colonel Johnson's Mercedes. She parked next to the Jeep and gestured to the gear in the back seat. "You get that, and I'll get what's in the trunk."

She popped the trunk and got out the weapons and her tool case, the one that Preston had been so suspicious of. She was halfway to the plane when Preston relieved her of the larger of the two bags. "You don't have to carry it," she protested as he shifted his weight to accommodate the heavy weapons.

"I'll manage."

They climbed the foldout stairs and ducked into the cabin where Colonel Johnson and Jazz were already seated at the meeting table.

Sabina smiled inwardly.

While she held Colonel Bustamante in the highest regard and enjoyed doing missions with him, Lieutenant Colonel Barbara Johnson had a special place in Sabina's heart. An RN by trade, Colonel Johnson had trained right along with the men over the years and had gone into black ops work when her son went off to college. After raising him by herself as a single parent, she went above and beyond in curing her empty nest syndrome.

She'd earned the respect of the entire detachment and was one of the finest officers Sabina had ever had the pleasure of working for. But as nice as she was, she didn't take shit from anyone.

It was going to be fun watching her deal with Preston.

Colonel Johnson smiled briskly at Sabina before turning to Preston, looking him up and down dismissively. "You can put the stuff back there." She motioned to the back of the cabin with her thumb.

Preston stiffened at the colonel's abruptness. Uh-oh. Colonel Johnson hadn't forgotten Kieran Lavigne either. Neither had Jazz, if the *fuck you* expression he graced Preston with was any indication.

A baffled-looking Preston stowed the duffles and weapons kit in the back. Sabina did the same and sat at the conference table. A moment later he sat beside her. The cabin door opened, and Captain Jimmy "Eagle" Begay stepped in.

"Mornin', everybody."

He tossed his duffle and weapons bag in the back and sat down on the other side of Jazz. He smiled genially around the table until he got to Preston. Then his smile faded, and he looked at him coolly.

Eagle was another alumnus of the failed rescue mission and, as a proud Navajo, had been subjected to prejudice all his life, as had Jazz and Colonel Johnson.

If the last member of the team was Paco Morales, as she suspected it was, things were really going to get interesting. Paco had taken all kinds of shit over the years, both as a dark-skinned Latino and as a gay man. He hated prejudiced *muthafuckas*—his favorite term—with a passion.

She hid her grimace. If it weren't for the Lavigne family, she could almost feel sorry for Preston about now. He was going to find this mission damned uncomfortable.

Paco ducked into the plane two minutes later. The colonel looked at her watch. "Well done, team. We're wheels up in five minutes. Take care of business and get coffee if you want it. We have a long ride and a lengthy meeting ahead."

Sabina slipped out of her chair and headed for the tiny restroom in the back. Jazz and Preston rose and headed for the coffee. She was coming out when she spotted the two men standing next to the galley. Jazz had his hand fisted and was up in Preston's face.

Well, hell. She wouldn't put it past Jazz to knock Preston on his ass.

She started to them, but the colonel beat her to it. "Stand down, Sergeant Washington. You're on American soil."

Jazz immediately backed away. "Yes, Colonel Johnson." He picked up his coffee and stalked to the table.

Preston poured a cup and looked at Sabina. "What the hell was that all about?" he whispered tersely.

"Same thing the Army was mad at you about last month. Classified."

He sat down. "Fuck that."

They strapped themselves in as the little jet's engines rumbled, and the pilot taxied into position. After a ride down the surprisingly smooth runway, the jet lifted into the air.

Colonel Johnson waited until the plane had leveled out before she passed around thin folders. "These are for you to study on the way down." She looked at Preston. "They stay on the plane." She then handed each of them a packet of documents. "Mr. Ramos, memorize everything in your packet. You and Sergeant Kaslov will also need to make up a cover story regarding your fictitious relationship."

Preston nodded.

"A few salient points about the emerald trade," Colonel Johnson continued. "The mines are owned mostly by the government, but corruption is rife, and not a whole lot is done to stop it. Emerald smugglers, known as *guaqueros*, poach the mines. By day they scour the riverbeds and scavenge the handful of private mines for overlooked stones. By night they rob safe houses where the stones are kept before shipment. The *guaqueros* compete with one another for the same loot."

"And nothing is done to stop it?" Paco asked.

"It's monitored by the National Police, who have their own corruption problems, and arrests are few and sentences are short.

"What makes it worse is that a lot of the profit is used to fund the so-called Green Wars, the violence accompanying the illegal activity, among other things. In your packets I've included some more information about emeralds tailored to your respective roles in this mission.

"Paco, Eagle, as *guaqueros*, yours is the most detailed. You'll need to be able to distinguish between crystalline, non-crystalline stones, and quality stones from the not so wonderful. Pictures are included of the desirable versus less desirable shades of color.

There's also a detailed step-by-step of the mining process, including the points at which theft and corruption occur.

"Jazz, yours and mine deal with the finished product and how to tell a good stone from a bad after cutting and polishing. Sabina and Mr. Ramos, just an overview for the two of you."

Colonel Johnson gave them a few minutes to look through their documents.

Sabina read through hers. Delores Casiano. Thirty-two years old. Resident of Richardson, Texas. An address in a nondescript middle-class neighborhood. Height and weight were a match to hers. The picture was different from each that'd appeared on her bogus IDs over the years. Three credit cards she knew from experience really worked. A health insurance card that would work too, in case of an emergency. A bit more of this and that a tourist might have in her wallet, including a wad of American dollars and Colombian pesos.

She peeked over at the driver's license in Preston's hand. Hmm. He was Humberto Casiano, age thirty-nine, same address.

He looked over at her. "Looks like you've acquired a husband."

"And I've acquired a sugar mama," Jazz crowed.

Colonel Johnson ignored Jazz. "The plan is detailed in your folders, but in short it's this: we separate into three groups when we get to Cartagena. Sabina and Mr. Ramos are an adventurous couple on vacation. They've learned they have old friends in Colombia they'd like to get in touch with for dinner.

"Mr. Ramos, stay in character, and do not in any way indicate that either of you is related to the men you are trying to contact. Paco and Eagle are *guaqueros*. Shady dealers in raw stones seeking to obtain uncut emeralds to pass along. They'll use this cover to see who is initiating the illegal process at the mining level.

"Jazz and I are wealthy jewelers out of Houston who aren't too concerned with the legality of the stones we obtain."

"Are you really gonna be his sugar mama?" Eagle asked slyly.

Colonel Johnson made a production of looking Jazz up and down. "It's either that or he poses as my son."

"And I'm too old, and you look too good for anybody to believe I'm your son," Jazz said smoothly.

Colonel Johnson snickered. "Suck up. Sugar mama it is," she said wryly.

She spent a few more minutes giving them a little more instruction, like the exchange rate of dollars to Colombian pesos, but they were a seasoned group of warriors used to working undercover and thinking on their feet. She trusted them.

They folded up the table, and the men turned their chairs around. "Sabina, you and Mr. Ramos need to come up with your backstory," Colonel Johnson said. "Take him through it in detail."

Sabina and Preston adjusted their chairs so they were side by side. She opened the folder and got out a piece of blank paper. "What do you do for a living?" Sabina asked.

He looked at her. "You know what I do. I'm a cop."

"No. What does Humberto Casiano do?"

Preston thought a minute. "Depends on how wealthy he…we're supposed to be. Are we middle class or floating in it?"

"Middle class."

"He's a car salesman."

"She's an accountant for the dealership. We met at the dealership where we used to work. We've only been married for a year, and we're not especially interested in a family. Not that I expect to need that kind of detail, but you never know. Is he fluent in Spanish?"

"*Hablo español con fluidez.*"

"You're fluent? I'll be damned. I didn't think you spoke a word."

His brows drew together. "My parents speak both languages without an accent in either and taught us to do the same. How about our buddy Delores?"

"*Hablo español con fluidez. También romaní.*"

"Romani's a language too?"

She lifted her chin. "Yeah. The language of my people. An Indo-Aryan language spoken by nearly six million of us. My parents taught us. It's the only thing from their old lives they preserved."

He looked around at the other soldiers. "They all speak other languages too?"

"Of course. We each speak three or more. Jazz and the colonel both speak Spanish, and she speaks the Haitian French of her grandmother. I think his third language may be Indonesian. Paco and Eagle speak Spanish, and Eagle speaks Diné. That's Navajo. His grandfather was a code talker. Paco learned Portuguese for when we work in Brazil. I speak fluent Russian, since Romani isn't too useful."

"Interesting."

They added a few more details to their backstory before studying the briefing given in the folders. About halfway through the five-and-a-half-hour flight, Colonel Johnson passed out sandwiches and chips that they washed down with sodas.

Sabina stared out the window at the deep blue waters of the Caribbean and wished she was going on vacation and not on a mission with a man she didn't trust.

They reviewed their backstory a few times, then returned to their briefing folders. Eventually, the small aircraft began its descent.

Preston leaned over and looked out the window. "I don't see the city anywhere."

"We're landing at an out-of-the-way airstrip, like the one we took off from. If it's the one we used before, it's a pretty good distance outside Cartagena."

"It's hilly down there," Preston said, and Sabina nodded. "Does the pilot file a flight plan?"

"He does. Don't worry. He has a cover story regarding who we are and what we're doing in Colombia."

The landscape rushed by as they flew into the country. Sabina spotted a short runway visible in the desert scrub. "Down there."

"It's not jungle."

"No. Northern Colombia gets maybe twenty inches of rain a year."

"I thought it was like in the movie. The one about a writer and emeralds."

"Since when is Hollywood to be believed? The jungles and rain forest are down close to the Brazilian border. Bogotá is chilly, even though it's close to the equator, because of its altitude. We may have to go there. It's closer to the emerald mines, and a likely destination for our brothers."

"Thanks for the geography lesson."

"Not a problem."

"So how do we get to town?"

"There'll be vehicles waiting."

They watched out the window as the small jet approached the runway. The pilot expertly touched down, and they bounced along the less-than-pristine airstrip. They came to a stop, and the team rose one at a time and shook the kinks out of their joints and muscles.

They each retrieved their weapons bags and duffles. Preston looked at them all carrying their weapons bags. "I gather I don't get one of those."

"You don't."

The pilot dropped the foldout steps, and they climbed out. Three cars waited alongside the runway: a beat-up old Jeep, a sleek late-model Lexus, and a rental-car type Mazda. "I guess the Mazda's ours," Preston said.

"Most likely."

They were about to head toward their car when Jazz turned to the colonel. "Is it okay now?"

"You're not on American soil anymore."

Oh, shit.

Jazz grabbed Preston's arm and wrenched him around. He raised his fist and slammed it into Preston's jaw, knocking him on his ass.

Preston leaped to his feet and raised both his fists, but Jazz was flanked on one side by Eagle and the other side by Paco.

Preston looked at the three of them. "If I throw a punch, the three of you are going to wade in and beat me to a pulp, so I'm not giving you the satisfaction. But I'd like to know what the fuck that was about."

"It's classified," Jazz snapped.

"Oh, *hell* no. The Army has thrown that classified shit at me for the last time. You either tell me what I did to piss you off so badly or get the fuck over it right now."

Colonel Johnson turned to Sabina. "Tell him," she commanded. "He needs to know what he did."

Sabina nodded. "It'll be my pleasure." She turned to Preston. "The night you detained me, took me downtown and wouldn't let me call anyone, I was due to get on a plane for a last-minute emergency mission in Mexico.

"We had five hours to effectuate a rescue or a vicious gang was going to assassinate the family of the consulate emissary. The kidnappers demanded a Russian-speaking go-between, and since I'm the only one who speaks Russian, they had to wait for me.

"Thanks to you, we didn't make our deadline. The emissary's wife, sister-in-law, and eight-year-old son were murdered, and the kidnappers got away.

"We had to retrieve the bodies and inform the emissary our mission failed and his family was dead. Because of *you* and your fucking prejudice against me and mine, they're all dead, Preston."

Tears of rage welled in her eyes, and she viciously swiped them away. "Eight years old, and he'll never see nine because of *you*."

Preston blanched. He looked around at the rest of the team, his face drawn and disbelieving.

"Every one of us was on the mission," the colonel said coldly. "Maybe you'd like to see what your prejudice against the Romani caused that night."

She motioned to Sabina, who pulled out her phone. "Here. Take a good look, asshole." Sabina scrolled down, then shoved the phone in his face. "See those bodies? Those murders could've been prevented if you hadn't done what you did."

Preston turned green as he looked at the picture of Kieran Lavigne, his mother, and his aunt. All beautiful, but for the bullet holes marring their foreheads.

"We could've saved them if we hadn't had to wait for the sergeant." Sabina made him look for a couple more minutes before putting the phone back in her pocket.

"Now do you understand what you caused, you motherfucker?" Jazz spat.

"Prejudice is a damned ugly thing," Paco said. "You're a minority. You know damn well how it feels, and yet you do it to others. What kind of asshole does that make you?"

Eagle looked at him with contempt. "You have their blood on your hands."

Preston's expression was vacant, his eyes glassy, and his entire frame seemed to fold in on itself.

He'd been shown, literally, what his prejudice had caused.

Sabina wondered if it would cause him to change.

She wouldn't bet her next paycheck on it.

Chapter Eight
Preston

Preston swallowed down the bile in his throat, the question ringing in his ears.

Do you understand what you caused?

He looked at the group of pissed-off faces in front of him. "I'm so, so sorry. I...I didn't know." He turned to Sabina. "Why didn't you tell me?"

"I *did* tell you," Sabina snapped. "I told you I had someplace I had to be and something I needed to do. Desperately. I *begged* you to let me go, or at least make a phone call. You refused. You wouldn't give me my phone, and you refused to let me go."

"You didn't tell me you were supposed to rescue somebody."

"Yeah, right. Like you would've believed me. And how, asshole, was I supposed to let you know when it was a matter of national security? To you, I was dishonest and loyal only to my own. Let's see. What else did you say to me that night?"

"Damn it, I didn't know lives were at stake."

"You shouldn't've had to know," Colonel Johnson said evenly. "The bottom line is your actions that night cost three innocents their lives. Emissary Lavigne lost his entire family because of you. No amount of money in the world justifies their loss."

"But...but—"

"Shut up, Mr. Ramos. That's an order."

"Yes, Colonel. But before I shut up, I have one question: am I going to be dodging their fists for the entire mission?"

Colonel Johnson turned to the three men. "Gentlemen?"

"I got it out of my system," Jazz said. "Even if I still think he's an ass-wipe."

Eagle looked Preston up and down. "I've worked with lots of assholes in my time. He's just one more."

Paco nodded. "Some people can't help being jerks. He seems to be one of them."

From where Preston stood, now knowing what he knew, he'd had it coming.

The picture the colonel made him look at swam before him. If he was sickened by a mere image, how much worse must it have been for them, having to recover the bodies and inform the next of kin, knowing the deaths had been needless?

Deaths that were on him.

On him.

His stomach lurched, and he ran for the edge of the airstrip. He barely made it before the sandwich and soda came roiling up. He heaved and puked for long minutes, the retching continuing long after his stomach had emptied.

He looked around, but none of them seemed inclined to help him, so he wiped his face as best he could and climbed in the Mazda beside Sabina.

"Your stuff's in the back," she said tersely.

He sat quietly as she headed down the rutted dirt drive.

Jazz and the colonel were almost out of sight, and the other two were even farther ahead on the almost-nothing track.

They bounced through a thin growth of desert-like plants. The dusty drive was so narrow the little car barely cleared the scrubby vegetation encroaching on the rutted tire tracks.

Sabina took the drive as fast as she could without bouncing them against the ceiling, which was to say not fast at all.

Preston's already sour stomach twisted and lurched. If there'd been anything left, it would be coming up about now.

The weight of what he'd inadvertently caused weighed heavily.

He doubted he'd get much sleep for a long time.

After what seemed like forever, they came to slightly better crossroads. Sabina turned right. They began to make marginally better time on the road and, in about ten miles, came to a small village. Not much more than a wide spot in the road, with only a couple of dogs as evidence of life.

"Is all of Colombia like this?" He squinted at the old, broken-down shacks leaning into the road.

"No. Cartagena's as modern as any city in the United States."

They left the village, and in a few miles, the dirt road intersected a two-lane highway. She pulled onto the highway and hit the gas. The farther they drove, the more their silence weighed on him.

He couldn't stand it any longer.

"I am truly sorry," he said softly. "If I'd known, or even had an inkling of what was at stake, I wouldn't have done what I did."

Sabina was silent for a long moment. "As the colonel said, you shouldn't've had to know. What you did was wrong in every way it could be wrong, and innocent people died."

"I know. That picture's gonna haunt me for a long damned time."

"But is it going to make any difference? Are you going to think about it the next time you're in a position to act on your prejudice, or is the next Romani you encounter going to be treated the same way I was? Is the next innocent family member going to be squeezed and pressured the way you did me?"

"I hope I've learned something."

Sabina was quiet for a while. "What about the other?"

"The other what?"

"Using your position in SAPD to investigate things for your father. And don't tell me you don't do it, because you do. You already knew who I was when you thought I was breaking into someone's apartment. The only way you could have known was if you used your connections in the police department to investigate the rest of Dominic's family. Are you going to keep that up too?"

"That's different," Preston said firmly.

"No, it's not. It's just as fucking wrong as the prejudice. You're abusing your authority."

Preston didn't try to hide his sigh. "It's not. All cops do it at one time or the other. My father believes I owe him because I didn't take over the company, and he thinks nothing of asking me to use my position to look into things for him. I try to put him off, but when he said Romani and ten million, I said I'd help him. That's a damned lot of money missing. I thought it was important to find out where it went."

"More important than the three lives lost, of course," she spat out.

"Damn it, no. I didn't know lives were at stake, and you didn't tell me. Look, I was in the wrong. I admit it and feel like shit about it. I would give anything to take it back and do everything differently. But I'm not the only one at fault for what happened.

"We're down here because your brother has my brother here against his will, getting mixed up in illegal emerald trading. And that was after swindling a shit-pile of money out of my dad's company."

Sabina laughed. "My brother has yours down here against his will? What a crock of shit. Preston, get over it. I know damned well Dominic's no angel. But you saying your brother's down here against his will is complete bullshit. He and Dominic are up to their eyeballs in this thing together. And something else for you to think about: has it occurred to you or any of your family that Jeremy might be in on the swindle? He might have cooperated with Dominic? Let my brother help himself to the money for a cut? Surely your brother's not as stupid as he seems."

Preston's jaw dropped. "He wouldn't do something like that. Dad made him a company vice president and pays him a salary commensurate with the position."

"Big whoop. If he's like Dominic, it's never enough. No matter what he has, he wants more. This emerald business is a good example. It's dangerous as hell, but if they pull it off, there's a *lot* of money involved in emerald smuggling."

"He wouldn't. And he sure wouldn't be down here willingly putting his life on the line for money. Jeremy has a strong sense of self-preservation. He's not going to risk his neck, no matter how much money's involved."

"Don't kid yourself. Hell, even your father was willing to concede he might not be all that innocent."

Which was why their father had insisted Preston come. But he'd be damned if he told her.

He shrugged. "I guess we'll see who's right about Jeremy."

Her eyes flashed fire. "And it ain't gonna be you."

Preston looked away from the heat in her eyes. It shouldn't be a turn-on, her anger and her passion. She was no friend of his or of his family. She was out to paint his brother in the worst possible light.

But like a teenager, he was growing hard, unbearably aroused by the sparks that flew from her as she expertly whipped the Mazda around a slow-moving truck and sped down the highway.

He fought to kill the attraction he felt for her, the desire to run his fingers through her thick black hair and plant a kiss on her oh-so-tempting lips.

His eyes drifted lower, taking in the curve of her waist and the flare of her hips in her cargo pants, and the way the brightly colored knit top encased her high, firm breasts. This was the first time he'd ever seen her in anything other than DCUs, and the civvies enhanced her already considerable appeal.

He wondered if he could seduce her. Probably not. He was convinced she wasn't into him. That she actually detested him.

But it would be a helluva note if she was.

They came to a small town, bigger than the first village, but not by much. The streets, if they could be called streets, were packed dirt, and the cinderblock houses were small and mostly devoid of grass and shrubs. Gaily painted murals brightened the walls, and a statue graced the main square.

A few of the villagers were out and about, hanging out wash or riding their bicycles through the dusty streets. Preston looked at the villagers closely. Every one of them was of African descent.

"We're in Palenque," Sabina volunteered. "It's the first free town in the Americas for African slaves. It's been here over three hundred years, and in two thousand five, it was declared a Heritage of Humanity site by UNESCO. The Palenquero language is unique to Colombia. I've heard different things about it. Some say it's Spanish-based Creole, and others say it evolved from Bantu."

"Huh. Are there lots of Black people in Colombia?"

"More in Cartagena than anywhere else. Jazz and the colonel won't stand out in the crowd. The Palenqueros have managed to preserve a lot of the African culture, like the clothing, the food, and the music."

"Too bad we don't have time to play tourist for real. I'd love to spend a bit of time here."

"That surprises me."

"Why? You thought I'd be prejudiced against them?"

"Pfft. Based on my experience with you? Yeah."

He opened his mouth to defend himself and snapped it shut. Considering her disastrous relationship with him so far, it was a fair assumption.

She glanced over at him curiously. "Where did you learn it?"

"Learn what?"

"Learn to be prejudiced against Romani. You weren't born prejudiced. You had to learn it somewhere."

"From my parents. Mom grew up on the same block as one of two feuding Romani families in Fort Worth. It got bloody and tainted the entire neighborhood. Dad's gone a round with Romani a time or two. I've heard about them more than once. And now your brother."

"What about your experience with Romani?"

"What experience? There hasn't been any."

"So everything you know about Romani has been secondhand, except for Dominic, who may not be guilty of what you suspect. Interesting."

"What?" he demanded.

"Interesting. That's all." She smirked a little.

Preston cringed. She was right. His prejudice was entirely secondhand.

But that didn't make it wrong. Or did it?

They rode silently as the Mazda sped toward Cartagena.

An imposing skyline slowly appeared on the horizon as they approached the city. From a distance it appeared sleek and modern.

"That place is huge. I'm glad Hal located their hotel before I had to fire him. We'd never have found them otherwise," he observed.

"We haven't found them yet. They may not be at the hotel."

"Wonderful. We could be here for weeks tracking them down."

She glanced over at him. "You and your father were the ones who insisted you come on this mission. Not us. If you don't want to put in the time, I can drop you at the airport."

"You'd love that, wouldn't you? No, I'm in it for the duration."

"What about your job?"

"SAPD granted me leave without pay."

"Must be nice to be able to afford to leave when you feel like it."

"Like hell. I'm having to pay my bills this month out of my retirement fund."

She looked at him. "Hit up your dad for the money. He's the one who insisted you tag along."

He stiffened. "I don't take money from my father. It's a point of pride."

"Seems kind of silly not to. He'd have to pay anybody else."

Again they fell silent as they made their way through the outskirts of the city. Up close, the city lived up to its promise: clean, modern, and bustling, with a skyline full of high rises overlooking the picturesque bay.

"We'll start with the hotel where your PI located them," she told him. "Did he give you the name or an address to put in the GPS?"

They pulled into a parking lot so he could enter the name of the hotel. They snaked through the increasingly heavy traffic to a downtown address. The hotel wasn't quite a fleabag, but it was hardly a five-star establishment. Sabina pulled into the parking garage next door, and they got ready to climb out.

She turned in the seat and caught his attention. "Remember, they're not our brothers. They're old friends, and all we want is to have dinner with them."

"What do we do if they've already checked out?"

"Leave that to me." She slung a large handbag over her shoulder and climbed out of the car.

Mystified, he followed her to the front door, capturing her hand as they passed through. "We're married, remember?" he whispered as she looked down at their linked fingers.

She nodded and smiled so naturally he would've thought it genuine if he didn't know better. Kudos to her. She was a talented actress and could play her role well.

He'd been right earlier when he'd thought he needed to up his game when it came to role-playing. Sabina's performance would be hard to top.

Swinging their hands together, they approached the desk. Sabina smiled brightly at the desk clerk. "We're looking for a couple of friends of ours who said they were staying here. Dominic Kaslov and Jeremy Ramos. Do you have their room number?" she asked in perfect American-accented Spanish. "We want to take them out to dinner."

The bored-looking desk clerk shook his head. "They're not here any longer."

Sabina smiled engagingly. "Are you sure? I talked to them no more than a half hour ago. They said they were still here."

"No, they checked out a couple of days ago."

"But that's not possible." Sabina pouted prettily. "They said to get their room number from you and knock on the door. Would you mind checking? Please?"

The clerk looked over at Preston.

"Sir, could you give us the number so my wife can satisfy herself that they've left?" Preston asked. "Otherwise I'm going to hear about it all evening."

The clerk looked from him to her. He shook his head and turned to the outdated computer. "They were in room four seventeen. Go knock on the door and see for yourself."

"Oh, thank you. Thank you so much." Sabina beamed happily as she tugged Preston toward the elevator.

She dropped his hand the minute the elevator door shut. "Whew, this place is a bigger dump than it looks from the outside. Which may be to our advantage. We have a better chance of finding something in the room if it hasn't been cleaned thoroughly."

"Ugh." Preston made a face.

She looked at him coolly. "I've bunked down in worse. If you really were a Ranger, you have too."

"I have. Doesn't mean I like it."

The elevator jarred to a stop at the fourth floor, and he followed her down the hall to four seventeen. Sabina whipped a small gadget out of the voluminous handbag and popped open the door.

"Slick," he observed. They slipped inside and shut the door behind them. The room had been vacated and cleaned. "Damn. It's cleaner than I expected," he groused.

"But there might still be something we can use. You're a cop. You know the drill."

She handed him a pair of gloves, and they started going through the room. He took the side closest to the doors, and she took the window side. They were quick but thorough, and Preston was about to give up on finding anything when Sabina came out with a triumphant "Oh-ho" and held up an old-fashioned matchbook. "Lookee here. I found it halfway under the desk. Chances are good one of them dropped it." She turned the matchbook over and peered at it. "Looks like an advertising giveaway. *'La Cerveza Fresca.'*"

"The Cold Beer. An original name for a bar. Why do we think this matchbook means anything?"

"About half the matches are gone, which makes for a good chance they picked this up in the bar. Dominic smokes like a chimney."

"So where is this bar? Is it somewhere close?"

She squinted at the matchbook and made a face. "It's a Bogotá address."

"So they went to Bogotá and then came back here? Strange."

"Not if they're looking for something or somebody specific, like the government official. We'll have to chase them down. We start with this bar."

"We're going all the way to Bogotá based on a matchbook?"

"Good point. Let's see what else we can learn. We can start with the clerk."

They resumed their pose as a couple and returned to the desk. "They aren't there," Sabina said, sounding really disappointed. "So much for taking them out to dinner. Do you have any idea where they might have gone?"

The clerk thought a minute. "I don't...no, wait. One of them asked me if I knew of any hotels in Bogotá. I don't, and I told him so. He said they'd find one on the internet."

Sabina thanked the clerk profusely, and they left the hotel together.

Preston sighed, resigned. "I guess we're trekking to Bogotá."

"No big deal. We were most likely going to have to go there anyway. The emerald mines are closer to Bogotá than they are to here. Eagle and Paco are probably already headed there." She looked at her watch and swore. "We'll have to fly. It's six hundred miles of hard mountain driving, and we don't need to waste two days in the car."

She whipped out her phone, and he listened as she arranged for Humberto and Delores to catch an early evening flight to Bogotá and to secure a car rental.

The commuter flight to Bogotá was uneventful, and there was another Mazda waiting for them. Preston slid behind the wheel as Sabina looked up the address in her phone. The sun had set, and the city lights sparkled brightly as they drove away from the airport. Preston pulled on a light jacket and was glad he'd thrown it in at the last minute. "From the air, this place is huge," he commented as he looked out the window.

"Over seven million people. Not quite as big as London, but almost."

"It would be easy to get lost in a city this size."

"Which may be part of why they came here."

They drove through city streets for nearly an hour, past a prosperous-looking part of town into a distinctly shabby neighborhood with narrow streets and rundown buildings covered with graffiti.

They located the bar and drove around the block, then parked along the curb in front of a boarded-up building. "It'll be a miracle if the car's still here when we get back," he murmured as they locked the doors. "I don't suppose you have a Plan B if it's not?"

"I always have a Plan B," she said coolly.

Of course you do.

They walked into the bar together. Heads snapped up, and the dodgy-looking patrons stared at them for a moment before going back to their drinks. Sabina glanced around before taking his hand and leading him up to the bar.

"Excuse me," she said in Spanish, smiling winningly at the bartender. "Have you seen these men?" She held up her phone, showing him first a picture of Dominic, and then one of Jeremy.

The bartender looked at them suspiciously. "Why do you want to know?"

Sabina went into her clueless-woman act again. "We're old friends. I really need to get in touch with them. We heard they like to come here and was hoping someone here would know where they are." She looked appropriately innocent.

Crap. Could she be any more obvious?

On the other hand, her act seemed to be working. The bartender's suspicion seemed to fade. He rubbed his hand over his mouth and took another look at the pictures. "This one." He pointed to Dominic's picture. "He was here a couple of nights ago talking to somebody."

"Could you tell me who?" she asked sweetly.

The bartender shook his head. "You don't want to know. Your friend...he is not smart. He was talking to a bad man. You don't want anything to do with this bad man."

Sabina appeared distressed. "Oh, no. I really need to reach them." She gestured to Dominic's picture with her chin. "My friend's mother is very sick, and I'm trying to find him so he can see her before she passes. It's important, sir. He'd really want to see her."

The bartender looked at her doubtfully. "This man he was talking to...he's a *guaquero*. A dangerous one. You don't want to tangle with him."

"You're right. We don't," Preston said gravely as Sabina teared up.

How the hell does she do that?

"But we also don't want to have to tell his mother he's not coming. We'll be careful. We don't want to cause trouble. We just want to find them."

The bartender thought a minute. "You never heard this from me, but the man he was talking to is known as *El Lobo*." *The wolf.* "Nobody knows him by any other name. That's all I can tell you. I don't know anything else."

"That's a lot more than we knew before. Thank you," Preston said smoothly.

"Yes, thank you," Sabina added.

The bartender looked at them solemnly. "Good luck. Be careful."

Sabina nodded. "We will."

They walked back to the car, which miraculously was still in one piece.

Preston slid in behind the wheel and looked at Sabina triumphantly. "See there? Your brother's the one behind it all. He's making Jeremy go along with whatever he's up to."

"Because he was the one talking to the *guaquero*? Get real. It proves nothing."

"It proves plenty as far as I'm concerned. If Jeremy's in on it, then where was he? Why was Dominic alone with the *guaquero*?"

"Buying groceries? Doing the laundry? In a different bar talking to another *guaquero*? Who knows? But you go on telling yourself your brother's not down here entirely of his own free will if it makes you feel better."

Preston would do exactly that. Not because it made him feel better. But because he was right.

***

Sabina

Sabina laid her head on the headrest. It was late, she was tired, and she still had to contact the rest of the team to tell them what they'd learned. Plus, she had to find someplace to stay that would square with their cover story. And worst of all? She had to cope with her increasing attraction to the infuriating man sitting behind the wheel, waiting for her to tell him what they were doing next.

Preston had to be the most hard-headed, difficult asshole she'd encountered in she didn't know how long, yet she still had the desire to grab him and plant a big, wet kiss on his lips. Which was a dangerous way to feel, since, as part of their roles as spouses, they would have to spend tonight, and every night in the foreseeable future, in the same hotel room and possibly in the same bed.

She was going to find the situation uncomfortably tempting. She hoped to hell he didn't feel the same way. If he did, they were in for a shit-ton of trouble.

She looked up hotel rooms on her phone. "The nice hotels are across town. We'll stay in one of those since Humberto and Delores wouldn't stay in this neighborhood. In the meantime, get back on the thoroughfare we came here on."

Preston wound his way through the narrow streets to the brightly lit avenue. By the time they reached the thoroughfare, she'd secured a hotel room in one of the neighborhoods of interest to the average tourist.

The hotel was near Plaza de Bolívar and was a definite relief after the seedy area they'd just been to.

Preston checked them in using his Humberto Casiano credit card, and they went up to their room.

Sure enough, a king-sized bed graced the center of the room. She heard Preston mutter something under his breath, but she was too tired to care what.

"We can either go downstairs to the on-site restaurant or call for room service," she said.

"Room service. I don't feel like being Humberto any more tonight."

"Fair enough. Menu's on the desk."

They settled on a couple of hamburgers and bottled water, and she called it in. Next, she put in a call to Colonel Johnson. "We chased a matchbook to Bogotá and hit paydirt," she explained to the colonel. "Dominic was spotted talking to a known *guaquero* who goes by *El Lobo* in a dive bar called *La Cerveza Fresca*."

"Good going for a single evening," Colonel Johnson said. "I'll pass the name to Eagle and Paco. Jazz and I spent the afternoon putting out the word we're interested in product and aren't too particular about its origins. We'll see if we get any takers. You and Mr. Ramos keep looking for your brothers." She paused. "Has the jackass seen reason yet?"

"No, Colonel Johnson. I don't think so."

"It's amazing how stupid some smart people can be when they want to be. Have a good evening, Sabina."

"You too, Colonel."

She clicked off and sank onto the bed. Preston sat down in the adjoining chair and touched his jaw where a faint bruise had bloomed. "Your buddy packs a punch."

"You were smart not to fight back. The three of them would have pulverized you and smiled while they did it."

"I noticed."

They stared at each other, the tension suddenly unbearable.

Sabina swallowed. She wasn't sure if it was anger or lust she felt, and she didn't want to find out. His eyes were wide, and a tiny pulse beat in his throat. *Uh-oh.* He was attracted to her, and it seemed every bit as much as she was attracted to him.

She hoped to hell the hamburgers got here before one of them acted on the attraction.

A knock sounded on the door a moment later. She jumped up and practically ran for the door, then smiled widely at the waiter with the covered plates. She graced him with a too-generous tip and set the tray on the dresser. Preston uncovered one and pushed it toward her. "This is the single patty with cheese."

She nodded and took the plate to the bed, where she balanced it between her legs. It had been a long time since lunch, and she was famished.

She dug into the burger and noticed with amusement that Preston seemed even hungrier than she was. It was no wonder. He'd upchucked his entire lunch after looking at the colonel's picture of the dead family.

She felt an uncharacteristic spurt of sympathy for him, which she quickly tamped down. He didn't deserve her compassion.

Still, she was glad he was getting something to eat.

They finished their burgers, and Sabina gathered her things and headed to the bathroom. She stood for long minutes under the shower, hoping the hot water would ease the strain of the long day. As the tension eased, lust took its place. She told herself she was a fool, that Preston was the last man on the planet she had any business desiring. That he was no friend of hers or of her family.

Now if her hormones would only get the message.

Cursing, she rinsed the soap from her body and out of her hair. She toweled off quickly and pulled on what she'd thought was a modest sleep tee and pants. But to her horror they clung to her damp curves, outlining her nipples and the flare of her hips, leaving nothing to the imagination.

She took a deep breath and left the bathroom, only to stop in her tracks at the sight of Preston barefoot and clad in only a pair of boxer briefs that showed her he had a lot to desire.

Her mouth went dry as she stared in shock. Time had been incredibly kind to him. His taut muscles and sculpted limbs were more in keeping with the body of a man in his mid-twenties, not late thirties.

Broad shoulders and a well-muscled chest tapered down to a set of washboard abs, with a thin sprinkling of chest hair that arrowed down and disappeared into the waistband of his boxers. Most likely, he was a runner. That ass and those legs did not belong to a man who sat in his recliner all night.

She felt her body clench and her core dampen at the sight of the nearly naked man across the room. It wasn't fair. This delightful specimen of man was an asshole.

A fact she'd do well not to forget. Even if he was looking at her with unmistakable desire in his eyes.

She motioned to the bathroom. "It's all yours," she managed to croak.

His lips set in a firm line as he nodded and brushed past her, then shut the door firmly behind him. He'd already turned down one side of the bed. She cautiously turned down the other side.

The bed was wide, and there were more than enough pillows, so she put a couple of them between her side and his.

Too wired to sleep, she went into her duffle and pulled out a paperback she'd started a couple of nights ago. But she couldn't get into the story. Instead, she kept sneaking peeks at the bathroom door and imagining Preston standing naked under the shower and wondering if what she saw of his package was as good as the promise.

Wondering if she'd have a chance to find out.

After what seemed like forever, he reappeared. His chest was still bare, but he had on a pair of pajama bottoms similar to hers. He rummaged around in his duffle and unearthed an electronic reader and sat down in the armchair.

"So what's next?" he asked as he powered up the reader.

"Us or everybody?"

"I guess everybody."

"Paco and Eagle will appear near the mines, posing as wannabe *guaqueros*. Now that they're armed with a name, they'll seek out *El Lobo*, since we know he has a connection with Dominic and Jeremy. Jazz and the colonel, in their role as buyers, will try to connect with the shady government official, and you and I will continue to look for our brothers."

"How do we do that?"

"Same routine as tonight. One of them has a dying mother, yada yada. It worked well enough this evening. I see no reason to change it."

"Do we show them both pictures or only Dominic's?"

She rolled her eyes. "Of course we show them both pictures. Jeremy's just as likely to have talked to somebody as Dominic."

"Not if he's down here against his will, he's not."

"Preston, shut the fuck up. You and your father are so out of the box if you believe Jeremy's here against his will. If he was really down here unwillingly, the minute Dominic had his back turned, Jeremy would be up and gone."

"Not if he had his passport taken from him."

She started laughing. "In that case he could go to the American consulate. For that matter, he could have pitched a fit at the airport and not gotten on the plane. Preston, your brother is down here because he *wants to be*. You need to get that through your stubborn head."

"I'll be damned if I get any such thing through my head."

"My brother may be behind it, but yours is at best along for the ride, and most likely up to his dishonest little eyeballs in whatever's going on," she snapped back.

Preston stood up and glared at her. "Who the hell are you to cast aspersions on my brother's character, considering what a lowlife yours is?" He stomped around the bed and leaned down until his face was barely an inch from hers.

"It's easy. I know *you*. You're a racist, prejudiced asshole responsible for three dead people because you had to fuck with the Romani girl. Your brother's no different," she snarled. "Furthermore, your father—"

Her tirade was cut off when his lips collided with hers. She stiffened for a moment, but the attraction she'd felt since she first laid eyes on him took over.

She pulled him to her, opening her lips and invading his mouth with her tongue.

Hungrily, desperately, they clung together as their lips fused.

He pushed her down and lay down on top of her, their bodies plastered together from head to toe as their fingers groped and stroked.

She snaked her fingers around his waist as he slid his arms under her shoulders.

His body was hard, his chest crushing her breasts, and his cock poking into the vee of her hips.

She opened her legs, and he thrust one powerful thigh between them.

They kissed and held on to one another, wrestling as they explored each other's bodies with greedy abandon.

A part of her knew this was madness and they needed to stop, but her desire for him and her need for release from the explosive tension won out, and she met him more than halfway. She was on a train barreling down the tracks full speed ahead with no brakes to stop them.

Finally, Preston raised his head. "Tell me to stop," he rasped. "Tell me to get off you, or I'm not responsible for what comes next."

In answer she shook her head and flipped them so that she was on top. "Is that enough answer for you?"

"Hell, yeah."

He reached for her tee and pulled it over her head, baring her pebbled nipples to his gaze. He palmed her breasts, holding them in his hands. "Gorgeous. Utterly gorgeous."

He fingered first one nipple and then the other, watching them grow even tighter.

She looked down at their respective pajama bottoms and rolled off long enough to remove hers. Preston had his off too, and her gaze was riveted to his jutting cock, even bigger and more impressive than she'd gauged.

"Do you have a condom or are we going to have to get creative?" she asked.

Preston nodded. He dove into his duffle and unearthed a condom, quickly covering himself.

He pushed her down into the covers and then he was inside her, filling her to the hilt.

They began moving together, heat and passion obliterating any finesse they might've shown otherwise. He pounded into her, and her hips pistoned in sync with his as they climbed to the pinnacle.

A soft scream erupted from her lips as her orgasm broke.

His followed immediately after, and they collapsed together in a spent heap. Her breathing slowed, and she felt his do the same.

After a moment he rolled off her and lay on his back, staring at the ceiling with a bemused expression on his face.

Shit, fuck, and damn. *What had they just done?*

She turned her head and stared at him uncertainly as a rueful chuckle escaped his lips. "Maybe we'd better table any further discussions of Jeremy's guilt or innocence," he said quietly.

"Probably a good idea."

He left the bed and disappeared into the bathroom, returning a moment later minus the condom. "Gotta admit, I'm embarrassed."

"Why? For giving in to whatever?" she asked, stung.

"Whatever was momentary madness and stress. Which was stupid on our part."

"Yeah, it was."

Still, his comment hurt. It was the truth, and she knew it, but it was still painful to hear.

"But that's not why I'm embarrassed."

"Okay, then. What's the problem?"

"It wasn't much of a performance on my part." His cheeks turned a little red. "I'm normally a lot better than that. I pride myself on giving my partners an enjoyable time, and you sure as hell didn't get one of those."

She shrugged. "I'm not complaining."

"But you're not thrilled either."

He tossed one of the extra pillows on the chair and turned to face her.

"Want a second go-round? I promise it will be better for you."

She looked at him disbelievingly. "You want to compound a colossal mistake by having another go at it?"

"We've already crossed the line. We can't take it back. No reason not to, I can see." He leaned over and captured her lips with his. "I've already fucked you. Let me make love to you properly." He lifted his head and waited for her answer.

"What the hell? Why not?"

She hooked her arm around his neck and pulled him down to her.

It was different this time.

Their lips met slowly and tenderly at first, but as desire began to grow, their kiss became deeper, wetter.

He scooted over so that they were side by side, their hands busy touching and caressing all the spots they'd missed the first time. He explored her body leisurely, skimming and tasting every crevice.

He paid special attention to her sensitive breasts, laving one and then the other until she was squirming.

Her hands were busy, too, as she acquainted herself with his hard waist and delectable ass. She felt his cock swelling, and she grasped it in her hand, caressing it until it was thick and hard in her fingers.

A part of her thought *no*. They were really playing with fire, but she would worry about it later. Right now she would revel in the touch of his lips and the strength of his body as he made love to her.

His lips trailed from her breasts to her waist and sank even lower. She tensed as he pushed her legs apart.

"You don't like it?" he asked.

"I…I do. It's just none of my other lovers liked to give it to me."

"Then they were fools. Open up, Sabina. Let me make you come again."

She opened her legs, and he parted her intimate lips with his fingers.

His tongue found and caressed her clit tentatively at first, but as the sexual tension rose, he became more demanding, sending her soaring as waves of pleasure crashed over her.

Her body shook with the hardest orgasm she'd ever had; the spasms seemed to go on forever.

He gave her a minute and began yet another sensual assault, this one even more insistent than the first, and in mere minutes she was crying out yet again with another wave of pleasure.

"So, so good," she said. "Can I return the favor?"

"I want inside you." He slipped on another condom and positioned himself between her legs. This time he entered her slowly, the leisurely capture of her body a slow glide into pleasure.

They moved together more gently this time, more attuned to one another's needs. It was less about themselves and more about one another, and she reveled in being in his arms.

They spiraled upward in tune with each other, no rush now, but still she crested yet again with his name on her lips.

He too reached the pinnacle, their bodies throbbing as they were swept up in each other.

They sank from the pinnacle, their response slowing and finally dying away.

Without breaking contact, he rolled to one side and lay facing her. He brushed the hair from her face and looked at her with an expression she couldn't quite interpret.

"Better this time?"

"It was."

"Good. I guess we'd better get some sleep."

She nodded.

He disposed of the condom and crawled in the other side of the big bed.

She was a little disappointed when he stayed on his side but told herself she was being ridiculous.

He'd been right earlier. The sex—he may've called it lovemaking, but there was no love involved—was a reaction to the heightened emotions of the last few days.

They were only blowing off steam, but they'd seriously complicated the situation by giving in to their desire.

She turned to face the wall. A couple of minutes later, she heard Preston's breathing deepen into the soft cadence of sleep.

What a shame. The best sex of her life, and it had to be with a racist asshole who hated her people in general, and particularly her brother.

Under other circumstances it would've been beautiful.

Momentary madness and stress they probably wouldn't give into again.

Another shame, but reality was a bitch.

Chapter Nine

Preston

Preston thanked the bartender and took Sabina's hand. Together they walked out of what felt like the hundredth seedy bar they'd been in today. "How many more tonight?" he asked, feeling like he was lugging around a two-hundred-pound weight filled with disappointment.

"There are a couple more Paco said the *guaqueros* like to visit. We can hit those and stop for the day." He glanced over to see her looking at him tiredly. "I know, I know. It's getting old. If it makes you feel any better, I'm as sick of this as you are."

"Seems like there ought to be a better way of tracking them down than this," he groused. "Checking out random bars and hotels. We could be at it for weeks. Hell, for all we know, they're no longer anywhere near here."

"Put a sock in it. We're not checking random bars and hotels. We're checking out known hangouts of the *guaquero* community and *El Lobo*. Paco and Eagle have passed on good intel." She checked her phone and pointed ahead. "The next one we need to check is up ahead. Close enough to walk."

Preston nodded.

They were in another rundown neighborhood he didn't relish walking through, but he doubted they could get the car any closer than where they were already parked. He knew his attitude sucked, soured by discouragement and fatigue.

He and Sabina had been putting in sixteen-hour days, sometimes even longer, visiting a parade of seedy hotels by day and dive bars by night, looking in vain for a couple of *norteamericanos* shopping for product.

Somehow Paco and Eagle had secured a list of establishments where the *guaqueros* hung out, and he and Sabina had visited most of them without having any luck since the first night—the night he and Sabina had fucked each other's brains out and then enjoyed some of the best sex of his life.

Which maybe was part of why he was in such a crappy mood.

There'd been no repeats of either the fucking or the delicious sex.

Tacitly, they'd agreed not to address Jeremy's innocence or guilt, removing the trigger that had set them off, and had settled into polite detachment, doing their best to behave as acquaintances or colleagues.

A part of him knew this was by far better than any repeats of their roll in the sack, but he was a healthy male, and she was an appealing woman he was sharing a hotel room with, and hell, he was sporting wood like a twenty-year-old.

It irked him to no end lusting after the sister of a man he held in such contempt.

They walked the block and a half to the next bar. This one was busier than the last, with clusters of roughly dressed men talking and laughing with one another.

They sidled up to the bar, and Sabina went into her looking-for-a-friend act. The bartender looked at the pictures and shook his head. "I've never seen either of them. But maybe Erica has."

He motioned over the scantily clad server. Sabina showed her the pictures. The tired-looking woman, who was on the high side of forty and trying not to look it, cocked her head to one side. "I haven't seen either of them. But I heard some men talking last night. There are a couple of *norteamericanos* sniffing around. Maybe they are your friends."

Preston forced himself not to react. "Maybe," Sabina said slowly. "Do you know where we can find them?"

"No. And the men who were talking about them aren't here tonight. Maybe if you come back tomorrow?"

Sabina nodded. "Thanks."

Preston kept his face impassive as they walked out. "What you want to bet those are our brothers?" he asked as soon as they were alone on the sidewalk.

"Seems likely," she admitted. "We need to check out the last bar and go back to the hotel so I can contact Colonel Johnson."

The last bar was a bust. They drove back to the hotel, and Sabina put in a call to the colonel and told her what they'd learned. She listened for a while before wishing the colonel a good evening.

"Paco and Eagle are already down at the mines a couple of hours away, and she and Jazz are coming here tomorrow. We're meeting at the Sanctuary of Monserrate at twelve hundred so we can talk without being overheard. She said both their teams have made considerable progress and we need to decide where to go from here." She slumped on the side of the bed. "You hungry?"

"Not with all the bar food we've consumed this evening. The arepas and empanadas are filling and damned good."

"Just making sure." She found her pajamas and disappeared into the bathroom.

Try as he might to think of other things, he imagined her naked body standing under the shower, hot water pouring over her generous breasts and running down to the vee between her legs covered by a soft layer of dark, silky hair.

Swearing under his breath, he pulled out the reader he'd stared at for the last five nights and wondered why he hadn't downloaded something more interesting.

Determinedly, he stuck his nose in the reader and managed to ignore her as she left the bathroom and climbed into her side of the bed. He waited until she was breathing deeply before crawling in his side and turning off the light.

Morning came all too quickly. They dressed in hiking pants and windbreakers, and again Preston was glad he'd brought some cool-weather clothes.

"What's the plan?" he asked as they got in the car.

"The church is surrounded by forest. We rendezvous in the woods. We look like any other tourists and have complete privacy, unlike a hotel room."

"Which could hypothetically be bugged."

"Give the man a cigar."

It was a long hike up the side of the mountain. "Tell me why people hike this trail when there's a perfectly good funicular and a cable car," he said offhandedly as they trudged upwards.

"Why do hikers like to hike? Because it's a passion for them. The devout will hike it as a form of penance."

He looked at her curiously. "Would you?"

"What? Hike it as penance? I guess if the priest told me to, I would. But it's not likely to happen. I haven't gone to confession in years."

"Catholic?"

"Greek Orthodox. How about you? Been to confession lately?"

"I'm not Catholic."

"Too bad. Confession's good for the soul."

"Methodists get square with God. We just do it differently."

"Whatever." She checked her phone. "The colonel's over there somewhere." She pointed into the trees before leaving the prescribed path.

He followed her through the thick woods, more alpine than tropical. They came to a barely there clearing, where Colonel Johnson and Jazz waited.

Both were wearing flashy casual clothes, and the colonel was wearing makeup and sporting a hairstyle in keeping with her role as an affluent jeweler.

Sabina nodded to the colonel, presumably in lieu of a salute. "Paco and Eagle are down in the parking lot. They'll be up shortly," Colonel Johnson stated.

The two men reached them five minutes later. They were dressed in rough work clothes, and both were developing deep tans on the exposed parts of their bodies.

"We'll make this quick before some zealous guard spots us and gets curious," the colonel said. "Sabina, progress report."

"We've checked out almost all the hotels and bars on the list you gave us," Sabina said. "We learned that Dominic was in contact with the *guaquero* known as *El Lobo*. All of this you already know. Last night a server told us there are a couple of *norteamericanos* sniffing around, talking to some of the players. That's all we've accomplished. I wish it were more."

"It is what it is," Colonel Johnson said. "Jazz and I have established ourselves as new players on the block. We've already been approached by several individuals about purchasing illegal emeralds, but none of the dealers who approached us have any connection to the government. But we figure eventually we'll be approached by this individual with product to sell. Paco. Eagle."

Paco nodded. "We've managed to pass ourselves off as *guaqueros* and have been frequenting the bars close to the mine. There's rumor of a big shipment of emeralds from one of the government-owned mines that's in the works for early next week, and a heist is being planned. The *guaquero* putting it together doesn't want to reveal himself to the official involved, whoever it is, and has set up a couple of *norteamericanos* to steal the shipment and deliver it to his place. With that kind of setup, it's reasonable to suspect the Americans will be eliminated after delivering the emeralds. There's no reason to think the *guaquero* has any intention of splitting the profits with the dupes delivering the stones."

"Those dupes being Dominic and Jeremy," Sabina murmured.

"Most likely," Colonel Johnson said. "The question then becomes whether the official in question will approach Jazz and me."

"Why would it make any difference if the official approaches you and Jazz? Won't you know who he is by then if Jeremy and Dominic have sold the emeralds to him?" Preston asked.

"Not necessarily. It's uncertain whether Jeremy and Dominic will still be alive at that point to tell us," Colonel Johnson said. "Chances are good they'll be eliminated before we can get to them."

Preston glanced over at Sabina. She stood impassively, taking in the colonel's words.

"You mean you intend to let the *guaquero* just kill them?" Preston was outraged. "You can't. They're American citizens."

"I know they are, and we'll do our best to save them. But our priority is the mission. It's a national security matter."

"It's bullshit, that's what it is," Preston snapped. "We need to step in. I don't give a damn what your orders are or if it's a national security matter. That's my brother, and I'm not letting him die." He turned to Sabina. "What about you? Are you going to let your brother die in the name of national security?"

Sabina took a breath. "Do you think I like this? I have a brother at risk, same as you do. But the colonel's right. We'll save them if we can, but we have a mission to carry out."

He gasped, shocked. "To hell with this shit. My dad was right to send me along. He said you'd throw my brother to the wolves if I didn't come along to protect him, and that's exactly what you're doing. I'll be damned if I let you walk away from them. I'm stopping it."

The colonel's face hardened. "You'll follow my orders. You were told before you came down here that you had to follow all orders, and you agreed. You'll abide by them, or I'll send you home."

"Orders, my ass. I don't have to follow your damned orders. I'm saving my brother."

In a lightning-fast move, the colonel whipped out a Magnum equipped with a silencer and aimed it right between his eyes. "You will do what I tell you to do. That was the deal you cut with Colonel Bustamante, and you will comply."

Preston stared at the gun in shock. "You wouldn't," he breathed.

"Don't test me. Savvy?"

He nodded numbly. Yeah, he understood. This bunch was not to be fucked with. The mission came first, lives be damned. He'd have to follow orders to the letter and hope to hell his stupid brother didn't get himself killed.

The colonel put the Magnum back in her oversized handbag. "Mr. Ramos, we don't want to see your brothers die, and I don't want to shoot you. Before you started with your bullshit, I was going to suggest you and Sabina observe from afar and make sure they're not eliminated along the way, and when push comes to shove, do everything you can to save them. But you are *not* to tip them off ahead of time or in any way interfere until we have identified the government official. Do you understand?"

He nodded.

"Sabina? Let me know if he forgets this discussion."

"Yes, Colonel."

Colonel Johnson turned to Paco and Eagle. "Do you know the location where the emeralds will be taken?"

Paco nodded. "What we don't have is exactly when the emeralds will be moved there. We may not be able to ascertain that until they're moved." He looked at Sabina. "It's over three hours from here. You and lover boy are going to stick out like sore thumbs. The mining towns aren't tourist meccas."

"Paco, I know it, and you know I know it. Thanks for the vote of confidence," Sabina said dryly.

"Sorry," Paco murmured.

"We'll be dressed for stealth," Sabina said. "And tomorrow, we'll switch out the sedan for an all-wheel-drive SUV. Do we wait in Bogotá until we get word?"

"You'll blend in better in the city," the colonel said. "Play tourist some more, but be ready to head out at a moment's notice. Jazz and I will keep up our charade in the hope the official will approach us. Eagle, Paco, let us know the minute the shipment's moved."

They all nodded. The colonel lifted her chin to Sabina, who motioned for Preston to proceed through the woods to the walking path. He could hear her footsteps behind him as he walked between the towering trees.

I wonder if she has a gun on her.

Stupid question. Of course she did. It was either in the backpack she carried or it was trained on him.

She'd been armed every time they left their hotel room, and he'd been fine with it. He just hadn't thought in terms of the weapon being used on him. Now he did and was fucking scared.

Preston shook his head. So much for his father's sage advice, delivered the night before he left, about protecting himself by making love to Sabina. He'd made love to her, all right, and she'd stood there and had done nothing when the colonel pulled her gun on him.

The more he was around her, the more he realized she was worthy of his admiration, not his contempt.

Too little too late.

Chapter Ten
Sabina

Sabina tucked her hair inside the ski cap and holstered her Ruger. The late afternoon sun would be setting in a couple of hours, and it would be dark by the time they arrived in the tiny mining town of Cachata. Paco had called less than thirty minutes ago, catching them playing tourist at the Iglesia de San Francisco. They'd spent the morning at the Museo del Oro and all day yesterday visiting other popular tourist attractions. While the sites were interesting enough, she was tired of sitting anxiously waiting for Paco's call and more than ready to get with the program.

Now the emeralds had been delivered, presumably the duped *norteamericanos* would move in and steal them tonight or tomorrow night. A part of her hoped the stupid Americans weren't Dominic and Jeremy, but she knew the odds of it being someone else were slim.

She also knew the odds weren't in their favor when it came to saving their brothers, unless the handoff was someplace they could access quickly after the government official revealed himself. She hoped to hell she and Preston could get to their brothers in time to save them. She didn't want her brother to die any more than Preston wanted to lose his.

They stashed her weapons in the car and headed out of town with Preston at the wheel. He'd been unnaturally quiet since his encounter with Colonel Johnson. It must've been a shock to him to realize he wasn't in charge, and that his life hinged on following orders.

And that he may not be able to save his brother.

But it was his own fault. And his POS father's. She'd hoped he'd take a plane home once he realized his interference wasn't going to be tolerated. But he'd stayed, surely in hopes of saving his brother once the emeralds were handed off.

That had to count for something about his character.

The road was narrow and winding through the mountains. "Good thing you switched cars," he said idly as they climbed up a steep incline leading to a switchback. Even the SUV struggled a bit on the steep road.

"Good thing we're both trained drivers," she added.

Still, it was rough going. They had the misfortune of getting behind a slow-moving truck for thirty miles or so. They finally got around the truck, but then the sun slipped behind the mountains and darkness descended quickly.

There was nowhere to stop for food, and Sabina was glad she'd thought to bring some energy bars, which they ate as they made their way through the inky night.

At almost twenty-one hundred they reached the tiny town. The GPS took them to a ramshackle house on the outskirts where Eagle and Paco were staying. "If this takes more than one night, we'll have to stay out of sight during the day," she said as they pulled up in front.

"Where do we stash the car?"

"That's Paco's problem."

They carried their duffles and gear into the house. Eagle was waiting with a big pot of stew and a pile of hot, tasty Navajo frybread. "You need to eat and then get over to the house. Paco's watching it now, but people here know his face, and we don't want to be compromised."

"Gotcha."

She and Preston dished up bowls of the savory stew and ate quickly. "What if they don't come tonight? Do we continue daytime surveillance?" Preston asked as he wolfed down the last of his meal.

"The chances are slim to none they'll break in during the day. This town is small, and everybody knows everybody. They'd be spotted instantly. Besides, the sooner they get the product, the sooner they can sell it."

She looked over at Preston. "Let's go."

He nodded.

They rendezvoused with Paco, who told them, "The house is three blocks over and two down. Here it is on the GPS." He held up his phone, and Sabina memorized the route.

The streets of the tiny town were quiet. It didn't take them long to reach the house, even more rundown than the one they'd just been in. Sabina motioned for Preston to take the back. He disappeared, and she hunkered down behind a wide tree trunk and waited. The air was chilly for being this close to the equator, and she was glad she had on a lightweight jacket.

At zero one hundred a five-year-old Chevrolet turned onto the street. The car pulled up in front of the house, as brazen as you please, and two figures in ski masks got out. Sabina wasn't fooled for a minute. Even with the mask obscuring his face, she immediately recognized Dominic's rangy form and characteristic strut. The other man was about the same size as Preston and moved the same way Preston did, leaving her in no doubt he was Preston's brother.

Any hopes she might have been harboring that the thieves were someone else died. The jewel thieves were Dominic and Jeremy.

Stupid fucktards.

Sighing, she waited until they'd disappeared into the house before grabbing the tracker out of her backpack. The coast seemed clear, so she left cover long enough to stick the magnet-backed tracker underneath the car where it wouldn't be easily detected.

She rushed back to her shelter behind the tree, but she needn't have hurried. It was a good fifteen minutes before the two emerged, Jeremy carrying a small canvas sack he tossed in the back of the aging Chevy. The two of them drove down the block and disappeared onto a side street.

Preston came around the side of the house a moment later. "I presume you put a tracker on the car."

"Yeah. We'll give them a thirty-minute lead and follow them, unless it looks like they're stopping for the night."

The tracker had stopped moving by the time they got back to Eagle and Paco's place. "They're pulled up in front of one of the local hotels," Eagle informed them, showing them the GPS. "You may as well grab a little sleep yourselves. It may be a long couple of days."

Sabina was more than ready to take Paco's advice. She curled up on the lumpy sofa, and Preston stretched out on a blanket-covered air mattress. Knowing an alarm would sound when the tracker started moving again, she fell into a deep sleep that went undisturbed. Four hours went by, then six, with no signal from the tracker. She was beginning to wonder if their brothers had discovered the device and left it in the hotel parking lot when it finally began to move at zero nine hundred. She and Preston had been up since zero seven hundred, and they were ready to go.

"They must not be in any hurry to make their money," Paco observed as they carried their gear to the SUV. He and Eagle had treated them to a big breakfast of eggs and more of Eagle's frybread.

Preston and Sabina looked at one another. "My brother takes his beauty sleep seriously," she said. "How about yours?"

"This is early for him. I don't think he's seen a sunrise since his last Boy Scout camping trip."

"I gassed up your car while you were on the stakeout," Paco said. "No telling where or how far you'll be traveling today."

"Thanks," Preston told him. "Much appreciated."

Paco ducked his head. "No problem." They got into the SUV.

"They were both decent," Preston said as Sabina slid behind the wheel.

"What did you expect?"

"I thought they'd want to take my head off," he admitted. "They were ready to beat the crap out of me if I'd punched Jazz."

"As long as you don't get in the way of their mission, they're not going to have a problem with you," Sabina explained. "Same goes for the rest of us. They got the pissed-off out of their systems on the tarmac." She checked the tracker's position on the GPS. "We may be driving most of the day, depending on where Dom and Jeremy go."

"If they're selling to the government official, it would make sense for them to head for Bogotá," Preston said.

"If the official's based in Bogotá. There are government officials all over the country, just like home."

"But what are the chances the official's in Bogotá? Pretty high, I'll wager. They'll go there."

"You're probably right."

He was. They followed the tracker at a ten-mile or so distance until it entered the Bogotá metro area. They got a little closer but remained out of sight as the tracker snaked through the suburbs and into the heart of the tourist area. "No more dive bars and fleabag hotels," Preston murmured as the tracker entered the parking garage of a luxury hotel.

"They think they'll have the money to pay for it," Sabina said.

"Stupid *pendejos*."

"I can't argue."

In their vehicle, they changed into the ordinary tourist clothes they'd stowed in the trunk, then spent the rest of the day on the streets around the hotel, their faces disguised with sunglasses and floppy hats in case one of their brothers spotted them.

The tracker didn't leave the garage all day, and they were about to give up on their brothers leaving when Sabina spotted them exiting the hotel on foot.

They followed their brothers to a café a couple of blocks away. "You stay here and watch for them to leave. I'm bugging their room," Sabina said.

"How are you gonna know which room's theirs?" Preston asked. "The stunt you pulled at the front desk last time won't work in a fancy place."

"A food delivery will."

She picked up sandwiches from a street vendor. The desk clerk made a production of calling the room, but with a little pressure, he caved and gave her the room number. She donned gloves and opened the door with one of her burglar tools.

The canvas bag was tucked in a desk drawer, its drawstring loosely pulled together. Sabina couldn't resist. She slid the bag open and poured out a handful of the uncut stones and stared at them. She knew damned little about emeralds, but as little as she knew, she could tell these were of the finest quality.

They were a clear, pure green, not too light or too dark, and even in their uncut state, their crystalline form was unmistakable.

There were few, if any, inclusions, and from their size, she'd bet at least some of them were going to be big even after they were cut.

She stared at the stones another moment before sliding them back in the sack and positioning it in the drawer as it had been before.

Their carelessness took her breath away. They had a perfectly good room safe they should've used. And the two idiots were still traveling under their own names.

They couldn't get much dumber.

So dumb they wouldn't notice a micro tracker or know what it was if they did notice it.

Sabina withdrew a pair of tiny trackers the size of a pinky nail. She took a quick look through their duffles. The first tracker she pushed all the way to the bottom of Jeremy's sunglasses case and held it in place until the adhesive set. She stuck the second tracker to an unused, inside pocket in Dominic's duffle. Given the choice, she'd have preferred planting them in a wallet or a phone case, but their phones weren't in the room, and there was no way she could access their wallets. At least this would alert her and Preston if their brothers changed hotels or left town.

She glanced around the room. The camera and mic were tiny, and there were any number of places she could conceal them. She settled on the top of a pole lamp. The little camera was wide-angle and took in the entire hotel room and was small enough not to be noticed, especially by two rank amateurs who weren't looking for it.

She picked up the sandwiches and let herself out of the room.

She and Preston could eat the sandwiches.

Sabina engaged in a bit of window shopping until Preston texted that their brothers had left the café and seemed to be headed for the hotel. She waited inside a small souvenir shop until he reported they'd disappeared inside the building. Only then did she meet him on the sidewalk.

They peeked at the camera, and Sabina stared in horror. Dominic and Jeremy were plastered together on the bed in a torrid embrace, kissing passionately.

"Holy shit," she breathed, handing the phone to Preston.

"What the *fuck?*" He stared down at the phone in shock.

They looked at one another. "Did you—?" they asked in unison.

Sabina shook her head. "I had no idea. Dominic's always dated women."

"So has Jeremy. He was even married to a woman for a couple of years. Not that being married tells you anything."

Sabina put away her phone, and they started walking toward their hotel. "A lot of people used to marry as a cover. Some probably still do. Or maybe they're both bi."

"Right now their love life's the least of our worries. Did you see the emeralds?"

"Sure did. They were in a bag in the desk drawer. Preston, there are tens of thousands of dollars' worth of high-quality product there. Maybe more. Somebody's going to be willing to pay a fortune for them."

"Which means they're worth killing for."

"We already knew that."

They returned to their hotel room. Sabina checked the phone. To her immense relief, whatever intimacy Dominic and Jeremy had been engaged in appeared to be over, and they were straightening up the room when Dominic asked, "What time did you say he was coming?"

"He said he'd be here by eight," Jeremy replied.

Sabina sat with her phone in her hand and fired off a text to the colonel. "Maybe now we'll get a look at this elusive official."

She and Preston kept watching the feed and ate the sandwiches. Twenty hundred hours came and went, and Jeremy and Dominic seemed to be getting antsy. There was a knock at their door at twenty forty-five. The duo admitted a well-dressed middle-aged couple who introduced themselves by first name only.

"Can we see the emeralds?" the woman asked, all business.

Dominic spread a towel on the desk and shook the emeralds out of the sack. The man got out a loupe and began examining the stones. The man took his time while Dominic and Jeremy waited patiently. Finally, the man named a price. It was a lot more money than Sabina had guessed the stones were worth.

"Is this your initial or your final offer?" Jeremy asked.

The man seemed taken aback. "It's my final offer, of course."

"I see." Jeremy appeared to be thinking. "It seems a little low to me."

The man's lips set in a firm line. "It's a good offer, and you know it."

"Tell you what," Jeremy said. "You think about it, and so will we. We'll speak again on Friday."

The couple nodded tersely and left the room. Dominic looked at Jeremy. "That was *a lot* of money you refused."

"Maybe. But we have three more people coming to look at them in the next couple of days. Let's just see what some of the others are willing to pay." Jeremy grinned lazily. "Now get over here, lover. Let's finish what we started earlier."

"Shit." Sabina clicked off the picture. "The last thing I want a ringside seat for is that." She looked over at Preston. "I know we weren't going to talk about it again, but it sure looks like Jeremy's the one running the show."

Preston shrugged. "Maybe it's a language thing. How's Dominic's Spanish?"

"He speaks it well. He was the one talking to *El Lobo*, remember? Truth, I don't care which of them is in charge. I don't think either of those two visitors was the government official we're trying to track down."

Just then the phone rang. "That couple was the Lagostinos," the colonel said without preamble. "Known fences of stolen goods, but neither of them has any association with the government. It appears your brothers are hosting a bidding war."

"I thought they were supposed to deliver the stones straight to the official," Sabina said.

"That's what Paco's intel said. It's not what they're doing," Colonel Johnson stated. "They're trying to get a better price than what he's offering."

"Which puts them in even more danger," Sabina said quietly.

"Absolutely. Especially when the *guaquero* who arranged the heist finds out the emeralds are gone," the colonel said.

Sabina took a breath. "Have our orders changed?"

The colonel paused a minute. "No. We still need to find out who the government official is. Let's hope those morons don't bypass the official and sell the stones to someone else. You and Mr. Ramos need to continue monitoring the situation, and we'll check out all their visitors. Let's hope the official will be among them."

"Yes, Colonel."

Sabina stared down at her phone. "They're on a fucking suicide mission, and they know it."

"Jeremy never did have a head for business," Preston said roughly. "If the *guaquero* wasn't gonna kill them before, he will now when he finds out they're trying to screw him over." He looked at Sabina pleadingly. "Please, isn't there anything we can do? Is there any way we can step in without jeopardizing the mission?"

"If there was, don't you think we would have done it already?" she snapped. "You think I don't love Dominic with all my heart? I think he's a fucking fool, but he's my brother. The thought of anything happening to him makes me want to puke."

He cocked his head and looked at her. "You say you love him, but you won't lift a finger to save him. So where does your loyalty lie?"

"You know where it lies," she said quietly. "I love my brother. But I took an oath the day I joined the Army, the same oath every service member takes, even if they never have to make a hard call.

"Because of the nature of the work I do, I've re-examined that oath on many occasions. I admit this is the first time it's been put to this kind of test. But I've had the training. The what-do-you-do-if-they-have-your-family training that every SEAL, Green Beret, and black ops service member is put through. A lot of soldiers get that far in the training and wash out, because they can't make the commitment."

"Obviously, you passed."

"As did every other soldier on the team. Even the colonels, who have sons who are the light of their lives. So, yeah, I'll do my duty and carry out the mission. Even if it costs my brother his life."

"You really mean to tell me your ultimate loyalty is to the military and not your brother."

"It is. Because, Preston, when you really think about it, fulfilling this mission is the right thing to do. Not protecting my brother's best interests.

"It's a shitty call to have to make, but regardless of what you think of me and my team, I'm loyal to my country, not only to my family or my fellow Romani." He looked at her, his jaw hard. "What about you? Where do your loyalties lie? With your country, or with your brother?"

"With my brother," he said instantly. "I'd like to think I'm a loyal American, but if push comes to shove, my brother, without question. I was one of the ones who washed out, by the way."

"The what-do-you-do-if-they-have-your-family training?"

"It's why I never made Green Beret. I couldn't swear I wouldn't break. There's no way I could let them kill a child or an innocent family member."

"And you'd sell out your country to protect a criminal. Even if he is your brother." He stared at her but didn't answer. "What a shame."

"It's how I feel," he said. "You know, damn few people would sacrifice a brother, a sister, or a child for the sake of their country. You and your detachment are the exception, not the rule."

"Fair enough. But whatever your feelings, you need to stay on board with the program."

"Don't worry," he said bitterly. "The colonel made her position perfectly clear."

"Please, Preston, remember it."

He shook his head. "Why do you care? You'd kill me yourself if I got in the way of the mission."

"It wouldn't be easy." Sabina raised her chin and looked at him. "To kill the man with whom I had the best sex of my life."

Preston blinked. "Really?"

"Really."

"Want some more?"

"I'm tempted. But we're the last two people who should be getting naked together. We have a lot of feelings for one another, and none of them are good. You have a burr up your ass about Romanis, and I'm a Romani."

"And you don't like me much either. You think I'm a racist asshole, and you think my feelings about the mission sucks. But, yeah, the sex was great. Probably the best sex I ever had. So"—he shrugged—"I wouldn't mind a repeat."

Chapter Eleven

Preston

Preston waited for Sabina to answer him.

"Knowing what we think of each other, you still want to have sex with me," she said slowly. "Interesting."

He sat down on the side of the bed and took her hand. "The attraction's been growing ever since we laid eyes on each other. Don't deny it. Can't explain why I want you, but I do. I want to touch you and taste you and be inside you." He picked up their joined hands and kissed hers. "I suspect you want the same, even though you won't admit it."

"I'll admit it. As stupid as it is, I want you."

"So? We had something special the other night. Let's try for a repeat."

They sat side by side for so long, he figured she was turning him down.

But then she turned to him and took his face between her hands. "It's stupid in the extreme, but I want you as much as you want me. Let's find out if it was a one-time thing or if it would be special for us again." She placed her lips against his and kissed him tenderly.

He let her kiss him for a minute without engaging. His way of letting her be sure it was what she wanted.

When she didn't break off the kiss, he put his arms around her and pulled her close, opening his mouth and deepening their kiss until they were fused together.

He let himself savor their embrace. No hurry tonight. Not if he had his way. They'd take their time, making each moment together a good memory.

He already knew the spectacular sex wasn't a one-time thing. It would be special every time he and this woman came together. Now he had to show her.

They kissed for long minutes before she pulled away. "We have on too many clothes," she said.

"Allow me." He pulled the gaudy touristy T-shirt over her head and removed his as well.

She reached out and ran her fingers through his chest hair. "Your body is bordering on perfect."

"Nah," he said, although the comment warmed him. "I'm thirty-eight, and my body looks and feels every day of it."

"You might feel it, but you don't look it." She grinned wickedly. "So how about you let me look a little more?"

He grinned, then kicked off his shoes and pulled his jeans and briefs down in one motion, leaving him naked to her eager gaze.

"Wow." Her hand drifted down his body. "Every bit as tantalizing as I remember."

He groaned as she grasped his cock. Not to be outdone, he reached behind her and snapped open her bra, revealing her generous breasts. Her dusky brown nipples tightened. In a motion like his, she kicked off her shoes and shucked off her jeans and panties, baring her body.

"Beautiful. Every inch of you," he breathed.

He took his time drinking in the sight of her taut, feminine curves.

While it was clear from the developed muscles she was in the prime of fitness, she was still every inch a woman, from her soft, kissable neck down to her ample breasts, to her nipped-in waist and flared hips.

His gaze dropped to the vee between her legs and the dark patch of hair. She had the beautifully curved legs of a runner, and from the muscles in her arms and across her shoulders, he could see why she had no trouble carrying heavy equipment.

Every inch of her body called out to him, and his cock tightened in response.

Oh, yeah. What they were going to do would be every bit as spectacular as it was the first time. Maybe even better.

He pulled her down with him, laying her across the bed on top of the covers. They began touching and tasting one another.

Preston was in no hurry, and Sabina didn't appear to be either.

They took their time exploring one another in a generous give and take. Her fingers were like fire on his chest and waist, her lips arousing as she kissed her way down his body, past the patch of hair covering his chest down to his stomach. Then her lips drifted further, torturing his cock with eager kisses before licking it as if it were her personal ice cream cone.

"Delicious," she teased as she took the tip into her mouth and sucked it.

He reveled in having her lips on him while her fingers squeezed his balls.

"If you keep this up, I'm gonna come, and I want to come inside you."

She grinned and released his cock with a pop. "Are you ready for me?"

"Are you ready for *me*?" He pushed her down on the bed. "Let's make sure."

He kissed his way down her body, starting with her swollen nipples, which knotted into tight buds under his lips.

She gasped as he parted her legs. "You liked this before, right?" he asked as he positioned himself between her open thighs, pushing them even wider, exposing her to his gaze.

He nuzzled her, feeling her dampen, before beginning a sensual assault that had her moaning as her body started to tremble.

He could feel her climax coming on, and he chased it, her body shaking under his as she came, her moans deep and loud.

He gave her a moment to regroup and began again, coaxing her into a second climax and then a third before sliding up her body, donning a condom, and slipping inside her tight body.

She clamped around him as he moved inside of her. He wanted to last longer, but he'd been craving this for days and couldn't help stroking faster, grabbing her ass and pulling her up as she arched and cried out as she came again.

He exploded, his cock jerking inside her as he spilled himself into the condom.

He wondered what it would be like to spill inside her.

They stayed wrapped up in each other as the tremors subsided, then he slid from her body and kissed her temple.

He grinned. "As good this time or was the first time a one-off?"

She smacked his shoulder. "You know it was every bit as good. Actually, better."

He chuckled. Yeah, it was better. Of all the women in the world, this one rang his bell.

"You hungry?" he asked. She nodded. "Me too. The sandwich barely made a dent."

He flushed the condom, and they put on enough clothes to be decent. They called room service and ordered an unfamiliar Colombian fish dish that turned out to be delicious.

She unearthed her paperback, and he got out his reader, and for once he was able to concentrate on the story.

She seemed to be enjoying hers, too, but stopped a few times to check the camera feed. Their brothers' room was dim and quiet. Faintly, they could see Dominic and Jeremy curled up together in the big bed.

"They're out for the night," she said as she put her phone on the charger. "We'll look in again in the morning."

She slipped off her robe and curled up on her side of the bed. Preston climbed in his side. "Come here," he said. She looked at him with a questioning expression. "Not for sex. I want you close."

She scooted over, and he put his arm around her as she laid her head on his shoulder. "Nice."

"Yeah. *Damn* nice."

Sabina relaxed, and soon her breathing evened out as she fell asleep. He'd thought he would too, but as tired as he was, their day crowded into his mind, making sleep elusive.

The news that Jeremy was sleeping with Dominic had shocked the hell out of him but didn't bother him. The shit with the emeralds had him torqued.

As much as he hated admitting it, Jeremy appeared to be running the show. Which meant Sabina's assessment of the situation was correct.

My little brother is in this shit up to his eyeballs.

Preston wondered why. The Ramos family was rich. When his mother had slipped and told him how much his father was paying the little bastard for basically doing nothing, Preston was pissed. Money wasn't Jeremy's problem. So what was?

If that weren't enough to keep him up at night, his conversation with Sabina kept running through his head. She wasn't the woman he'd thought she was. The more time he spent with her, the more he had to admire her unfailing strength and integrity to do the right thing.

That took an impressive amount of loyalty and a strong moral compass.

He and his family didn't share either.

His father had sent him on this fool's errand with one goal: protect Jeremy, no matter what he'd done or what he was guilty of. And, as he'd done all his life, Preston went willingly, determined to protect his brother at all costs. The only thing that stopped him was reality staring him in the face via the barrel of the colonel's gun.

He ran his hand down Sabina's arm and placed a kiss on her temple.

He was falling for her. Which was the definition of stupid. It would go nowhere. She didn't think a whole lot of him and had no use for him aside from a bit of great sex.

That and any feelings they could try to develop would crash and burn if this played out the way he expected it to.

Both their brothers could die on their watch.

Chapter Twelve

Sabina

Sabina sat on the side of the bed and watched the camera feed from Jeremy and Dominic's room. She and Preston had been watching the two of them for the last three days, growing more appalled by the day as the bidding war continued. If *El Lobo* didn't already know what they were up to, he would soon, and their lives would really be worth nothing.

Preston hadn't approached her to intercede, but she could tell he wanted to. And she understood. She was tempted, hoping this mission didn't cost her not only Dominic, but the entire Kaslov family.

She figured Preston had the same concerns.

He came out of the shower with a towel wrapped around his waist. His hair was damp, and a faint sheen of moisture covered his chest and legs.

"So what's new with our favorite fucktards?" He unzipped his duffle and unearthed a pair of jeans and a Bogotá T-shirt. "Thanks for doing the wash yesterday. I was wearing my last clean clothes."

"You're welcome. I was down to my last outfit too."

Preston dropped the towel, and she gave herself a moment to enjoy the view. He really was a gorgeous man, she thought as he pulled on a pair of boxer briefs. They'd become comfortable being naked in front of one another and had sex every night since returning to Bogotá. They now knew almost every inch of each other's bodies.

Colonel Johnson might be amused if she knew Sabina and Preston had become lovers. She didn't think the colonel would care as long as the mission went according to plan.

What wasn't going to plan was Sabina's feelings toward Preston. Instead of enjoying a simple hit-and-run affair, she was starting to care about the man, which was a disaster in the making.

Nothing else seemed to matter when she came apart in his arms.

Preston pulled on his jeans and tee and peered over her shoulder.

"They're just getting dressed," she said. "They've been in the shower together for a half hour or so."

"TMI."

"Sorry. You asked."

Preston sat beside her, and once the two men were out of the shower and dressed, Sabina refreshed the feed as they watched their brothers together.

Jeremy threw his duffle on the bed and started stuffing in dirty clothes.

"We're not taking the offer from yesterday?" Dominic asked as he tossed his duffle on the bed beside Jeremy's.

"We might. But we owe it to ourselves to at least see what this much-touted government official in Cartagena wants to offer us. Who knows? It might be even better than yesterday."

"And it might be a lowball figure if he thinks he has it sewn up with El Lobo. Jeremy, let's take the offer from yesterday and get the hell on a plane to San Antonio. I don't like jacking with that crooked bastard."

"No. I want to find out if the government dude would really pay more. If he would, then great. If not, we contact the dealer we talked to yesterday and sell to him." Jeremy put his arm around Dominic's shoulders. "Come on, Dom. Let's make as much as we can on this deal. With that and what I took from dear old Dad's company, we'll never have to work again. Now get your stuff packed, and we'll catch a flight to Cartagena."

Preston sucked in a sharp breath. "Fuck. Me. You were right. Jeremy did it. He stole from our father's company. The piece of shit muthafucker."

"I'm sorry," Sabina said softly.

"Yeah. Me too."

They continued to watch. "Shit. If they walk out of there and get on a plane, we're gonna lose them," Preston said.

"Not a problem. I planted trackers."

"You *what*?"

She grinned. "Jeremy's is in his sunglasses case, and Dominic's in his duffle."

Preston laughed. "Well, aren't you the clever operative."

"Not only can we track them, so can the colonel. She's had access to the camera feed too."

"Son of a bitch. Has she been watching and listening the same as we have?"

"You mean, does she know our brothers are lovers? Ah, yeah."

"I'm thinking she won't care about their love life, only their crimes."

"Her only son's gay. She'd never judge about that. The criminal stuff…she's pissed off, no doubt."

They packed and checked out of their hotel. "Do we retrieve the camera?" Preston asked as they loaded their stuff into the rental car.

"Yeah. The next guests may not be as oblivious as our brothers."

They swung by their brothers' hotel, and Sabina made quick work of retrieving the camera.

By the time they fought their way through the Bogotá traffic to the airport and turned in the car, Dominic and Jeremy were already on a flight to Cartagena.

Sabina secured the last two seats on the next flight, and by the time they'd landed, the trackers indicated Dominic and Jeremy were at another luxury hotel in the heart of the tourist district.

The stifling air slapped them in the face as they walked out of the airport. "Crap, this is miserable. I got spoiled with the cool weather in Bogotá," Preston groused.

"We're at sea level, that's why," Sabina said. "I have a car and a hotel room reserved here. It's only a couple of blocks from theirs. I need to get into their room with a camera. I'll plant it while they're out to dinner."

Since it was unlikely the duffle or the sunglasses would go with them to dinner, Sabina and Preston disguised themselves with hats and sunglasses, then waited until Dominic and Jeremy walked out of the hotel and into the parking garage.

This time Sabina used a pizza to find out what room they were in and again planted the miniscule camera. She and Preston returned to their hotel room and parked in front of the camera feed, munching on the pizza as they waited for their brothers to return from dinner.

At nearly twenty-one hundred hours the lovers came back.

"I hope to hell our potential buyer hasn't come and gone while we cooled our heels waiting for the damned kitchen to get our dinner," Dominic complained. "That's all we need. Some pissed-off government dude."

Jeremy laughed. "You think he's not gonna be pissed if we sell to somebody else? He and *El Lobo* both."

"I know, damn it. You think it's not scaring the shit out of me?"

"Dominic, chill. The minute we have the money, we'll head for the airport. We'll fly into Grand Cayman, drop off the money in the bank, do a couple of days at the beach if you want, and head home, a couple of rather rich young men. *El Lobo* will never find us. He's a big cheese here in Colombia, but his reach doesn't extend past the Colombian border."

Sabina shook her head. *These two idiots don't have a clue how organized crime works.*

"I hope to hell you're right. Any idea what time he's coming?"

Jeremy checked his phone. "Not for another half hour."

Sabina alerted the colonel, and with Preston settled in for a ringside seat.

She was jumpy. Finally, *finally,* they were going to get a glimpse of the Colombian official that had evaded two governments for so long, who'd been dealing in emeralds and shunting the profits to terrorist groups in the United States.

Maybe, once they knew who the official was, there would be time to save their idiot brothers.

At the appointed time, a brisk knock had Jeremy opening the door to a youngish man in ripped jeans and huaraches with hair down to the middle of his back. Jeremy looked first at the man and then at Dominic, and an unspoken message passed between them.

The same message that passed between Sabina and Preston.

"Hell and damnation. No way that clown is any kind of government official," Preston murmured.

"Damn straight." Sabina fought down the crushing disappointment and listened.

Jeremy admitted the guy to the hotel room. "Where have you been? You're late getting here with the stones. You were due three days ago," the young man said accusingly.

"And you're no government official," Jeremy shot back. "Who are you, and why aren't we speaking to our customer?"

The man seemed put out. "My employer doesn't deal in person with anyone from the mines. I'm his representative and fully authorized to deal on his behalf."

"Whatever." Jeremy shrugged. "Dominic, show him the product."

"That's one way to protect your identity," Preston observed.

"It's worked for him for years," Sabina murmured.

Dominic spread out the towel and spilled out the stones. The representative sat at the desk and turned on the crook-neck lamp. He got out a jeweler's loupe, and one by one, he examined the stones as Dominic and Jeremy looked on less than patiently.

The man said nothing until he finally raised his head. "These are good. Your supplier didn't exaggerate their quality." Dominic and

Jeremy waited while the young man examined the stones a second time. "I'm not at liberty to make an offer tonight. Not until my employer and I have spoken. But I promise you, the offer will be substantial. You will be here tomorrow?" They nodded. "And ready to deal?" The pair nodded again.

"You'll hear from me soon."

Jeremy let the man out, and he and Dominic high-fived one another. "Hot damn, did you see the look on his face when he looked at the rocks?" Dominic crowed. "None of the others looked at them like that."

"None of the others knew what they were looking at," Jeremy said smugly.

"Or they were savvy enough not to let on in front of you," Preston mused softly.

"I'll bet his offer's going to be double what the others were," Jeremy continued. He did a happy dance. "Good for you, government guy, whoever you are. We'll be on a plane to Grand Cayman by this time tomorrow with enough money to last us the rest of our lives."

"If the morons aren't dead by then," Sabina murmured.

"What about *El Lobo*'s share?" Dominic asked.

"If he shows up in time, we pay him. If he doesn't, oh well."

Sabina and Preston listened in for a few more minutes while their brothers congratulated one another and made plans for a rosy future.

Sabina fought down her disappointment. They hadn't accomplished what they had come for. The government official was still an unknown, and their brothers were still in danger.

Nothing more of interest appeared to be happening in Jeremy and Dominic's hotel room, and they were about to click off when Colonel Johnson called.

"Change of plans," she said without preamble. "We're going to reveal our presence to your brothers and secure their cooperation in determining who the official is."

Relief poured through Sabina's system with such force she had to stop her hand from shaking. Her brother's odds of survival just skyrocketed. "Yes, Colonel. How are we going to go about this?"

"We have a meeting with your brothers at zero six hundred tomorrow. We'll lay it out: they cooperate with us and help us find out who the official is, or we cuff them, take them home, and turn them over to the authorities. Even though they're acting down here, they're still breaking American law. There's also the ten million they swindled from the Ramos company they need to answer for. Can Mr. Ramos hear us?"

"He's right here. I'll put you on speaker."

The colonel laid out the plan. The entire team would converge on Jeremy and Dominic at zero six hundred the next morning, waking them from sleep and catching them off-guard. They would hear their limited options, which would give them no choice but to agree.

"Colonel, I'm not trying to argue with you," Preston said. "But my brother's hard-headed in the extreme. I'm not sure he'll cave."

"I believe that's why you're on this trip. To make him see reason. If you can't, I'll use the same argument with him I did with you. It's quite effective."

Preston nodded, and Sabina fought the urge to chuckle at the look of panic on her lover's face.

The colonel clicked off. Sabina and Preston looked at one another, neither of them trying to conceal their relief. "They're still in some danger, but not like before," Sabina said. "They may sit in jail for a while, but at least they'll be alive."

They set their alarms and went to bed, to sleep and nothing more.

The next morning, at zero five fifty, they joined the rest of the team in a hotel room down the corridor from Dominic and Jeremy's. They were a formidable bunch, Sabina thought as she looked at her fellow soldiers. They were all dressed in tactical gear and looked every bit as badass as they were.

Even Preston, dressed in camo pants and an olive tee, looked intimidating.

Their brothers would have to get on board once the colonel explained the reality of things to them.

If not, the colonel would let her Magnum do the talking.

They checked to see if the corridor was empty, and Sabina worked her magic with one of her breaking-and-entering tools. They filed into the room and surrounded the bed.

Jeremy and Dominic lay entwined with the covers kicked off, naked. Sabina could've not seen that and lived a happy life.

Paco snapped on the light, and Jeremy opened his eyes a slit.

"What the—" Jeremy yanked himself out of Dominic's arms and jackknifed up, pulling the covers up to his chin. "What...what the hell's going on?" He stared in shock at the soldiers surrounding them.

Dominic took a moment longer, but he too bolted upright and stared at them, zeroing in on his sister. "Sabina. What the fuck are you doing here?" He grabbed for the sheet and managed to cover himself up to his waist.

Jeremy turned to Dominic. "Your sister's here?"

Dominic looked around. "Yeah. And if I'm guessing right, the dude over there who looks like you is your brother."

Jeremy blinked and squinted. "What are you doing here, Preston? And who are the rest of these people?"

The colonel stepped forward. "I'm Lieutenant Colonel Barbara Johnson, United States Army. These are my soldiers. And you two gentlemen are in a world of trouble."

Dominic and Jeremy looked at one another. "What the hell do you mean?" Jeremy demanded.

"What the hell is right, you stupid fucker," Preston snapped. "You fucktards are in so much trouble you'll never get out of it. Way to go, dickwad."

Dominic turned to Sabina. "I haven't done anything wrong, sis. We're just down here on vacation. Honest."

"Shut your mouth, Dom. You wouldn't know honest if it bit you in the butt," Sabina ground out, not even trying to hide her anger.

"Honest? How about stealing a sack of uncut emeralds and holding a bidding war for stolen merchandise? You've been under surveillance for the past five days. We know everything you two pea brains have been up to."

"Which means nothing," Jeremy scoffed. "We're not on American soil."

"You're still breaking American law. I could give you the penal code, but you wouldn't understand it or its implications," Colonel Johnson stated.

"And what about the money you swindled from your own family's company?" Jazz asked with a wicked grin. "Daddy might not care, but you can bet the other investors will."

"He did it," Jeremy snapped, pointing to Dominic.

"Bullshit. It was your idea," Dominic shot back.

Eagle's lips twitched. "Honor among thieves. Don't you love it?"

The colonel eyed the naked men. "Instead of pointing fingers, how about you two start thanking us. If you'd delivered those stones today, you wouldn't've lived until sunset. *El Lobo* isn't about to share his profits with anyone, much less a couple of dumbshit *norteamericanos* down here hoping to get rich quick."

That appeared to take the wind out of Dominic's sails. Jeremy, on the other hand, looked at her nonchalantly. "We would've been fine. *El Lobo*'s in Cachata."

"*El Lobo*'s in a room on the third floor of the hotel across the street," Paco said. "Right where he can see out the window to the front door of this fine establishment. We tracked him there yesterday. The minute he sees your customer leaving with the stones, you two are history."

Jeremy's eyes widened. Dominic sucked in a breath.

Sabina blinked with surprise. She wondered why the colonel hadn't told her and Preston. Unless she still didn't trust Preston to be on board with the program.

"None of which is particularly relevant to our presence here. If this was only a matter of emerald smuggling, the United States government would've left you to your fate," the colonel said. "But we're down here for another reason, and guess what? You two gentlemen are going to help us do what we came to do."

Dominic nodded. Jeremy looked at her disbelievingly. "You've got to be kidding. Help you? I don't think so."

Colonel Johnson looked over at Preston. "He's as big a jackass as you are. Would you care to explain things to your brother?"

Preston bent down and looked his brother in the eye. "I threatened to defy her, to go over her head and do things my way, and she pulled a gun and pointed it at my forehead. I suspect she's got that Magnum with her this morning and would happily do the same to you. Shut the fuck up, Jeremy. You're going to do exactly what she says, and you won't be pulling any more shit. Otherwise, I'll be taking you home in a body bag. ¿Comprendes?"

Jeremy gulped. "Dad would never let her shoot me."

"Do you see Dad here?" Preston made a production of looking around. "Do any of you see my father?" He got a group headshake. "How about that. I don't, either. As you pointed out, we're not on American soil. These soldiers can do what they need to and not answer to anyone. Including Roel Ramos. That means you're going to do whatever the hell they tell you to do. Then you're going to go home and face the music, and hope you get out of prison while you're still young enough to get it up without a pill. Do. You. Understand. Me?"

Jeremy finally nodded. He looked at the colonel. "Can we at least get some clothes on?"

"Mr. Ramos, Sabina, find your brothers something to wear."

They went into the duffles, found them some clothes, and under the watchful eyes of the soldiers, Dominic and Jeremy dressed.

The colonel sat them down on the bed and pulled out the desk chair, pulling it up to face them. "Here's the deal. For reasons which are nobody's business but the State Department's, our government would like to know the identity of the Colombian government official.

"We've been tasked with finding out who this individual is. The best way to do this is a sting. When the official's representative returns, you will have suddenly developed a deep distrust of him and all other go-betweens the official might send your way. You're going to refuse to do business with him and insist on a face-to-face meeting with the official."

"What if it makes the representative or the official mad?" Dominic blurted. "It could get us killed."

"Mr. Kaslov, I promise you're a lot further away from dying than you were before we gave you your wake-up call," Colonel Johnson said. "It was a certainty, and now it's only a maybe."

"What makes you think the official won't blow off the deal entirely and walk away?" Jeremy asked.

"It's a chance we'll have to take," the colonel said. "But I watched last night as the representative examined the stones. We all watched. We saw the look on his face when he saw the emeralds. I think the official is going to want the stones badly enough to reveal himself to you. After all, the official is certain you're going to be dead in a matter of hours after the stones are delivered. Why should he care if you see his face?"

Dominic winced. Even Jeremy looked a little shaken.

"So we have to do the sting. Then what?" Dominic asked.

"You go home and face the music," Colonel Johnson said.

"What kind of deal is that for us?" Jeremy asked sullenly. "We help you and then go home to a prison sentence. Why should we cooperate with that?"

"Because your alternative is a body bag, courtesy of *El Lobo*," Preston said tersely.

"Gotcha," Jeremy said quietly.

Chapter Thirteen

Preston

Preston wondered if his brother had truly "gotten it." Based on past behavior, he was probably expecting Preston to bail him out of the clusterfuck he'd created.

Preston looked down at his brother and resisted the urge to reach out and shake him until his teeth rattled. The damn fool didn't know when he was beaten. He could see the wheels turning in Jeremy's head, trying to figure out a way around what was happening.

His brother was an entitled, spoiled jackass out for only himself. He'd have to answer for his actions, and Preston suspected an American prison would be a much better place for Jeremy to cool his heels than a body bag.

The colonel turned to Preston and Sabina. "I'm going to break protocol and let the two of you talk to these gentlemen. I suspect they're not quite on board. It's your job to see that they are. This sting has to go perfectly." She looked around at the rest of the team. "We'll give them an hour with their brothers. Jazz, park yourself outside the door. Anybody unauthorized comes through, shoot 'em."

The rest of the team sailed out, leaving Preston and Sabina with their brothers. The four of them looked at one another. "This is all bullshit," Jeremy said. "Now how are you going to get me out of here without that asshole shooting me?"

Preston raised his eyebrow. "I'm not. I'm not lifting a finger to help you. You're going to do exactly what the colonel tells you to do. And then you're going home and facing whatever consequences are coming to you."

"But…but I'm your brother. You *owe* me. Besides, Dad would expect you to."

"I don't owe you jack shit, and I'm not getting my ass shot by that woman because I didn't follow her orders. Now, are you on board, or do I tell them to truss you like a turkey and throw you in the cargo hold of a military transport for home?"

Jeremy looked at him disbelievingly. "Dad will never forgive you."

"No, he probably won't." Preston shrugged. "And I don't care. I'm more concerned with keeping you alive than I am about our father getting angry. Besides, it's Dad's fault you're such an ass-wipe in the first place. You're not my problem. You're his."

"What about me?" Dominic asked. "What's gonna happen to me?"

Sabina looked at her brother coolly. "I suppose it depends on whether you get on board with the program. If you start giving me the same bullshit your buddy's giving his brother, bye-bye. You're headed back to the States to face the music. I'm not here to save your criminal ass. I'm here to do my job, and right now, you're part of that equation."

Dominic sank into the bed and put his head in his hands. "I knew it was too damn good to be true." He looked up and glared at Jeremy. "I never should've listened to you, asshole." He looked from Sabina to Preston. "He thought the whole thing up. Not me."

Jeremy started to sputter. "Not true, and you know it. I had to come. I didn't have a choice."

"You didn't have a choice because you owe half the bookies in San Antonio," Dominic spat back. He looked up at Sabina through bleary eyes. "He thought it up. It sounded good, so I went along for the ride. It was like the stories Grandpa used to tell. It sounded like fun."

"Yeah. Real fun," Sabina said, sounding as disgusted as Preston felt. "How did it escape your notice the family decided years ago they would put aside the dishonest lifestyle and live like law-abiding

Americans? They gave it up and became honest citizens before I was born. Did it ever occur to you that maybe they had a reason for changing their ways?"

Dominic lifted his chin. "Uncle Milo doesn't seem to mind."

"Uncle Milo runs his mouth a lot and has a good laugh, but he has a legitimate job. He's not out scamming old ladies or stealing emeralds." She held Dominic's gaze. "Are you on board, or are you going to try something that's gonna get you killed?"

"I'm on board," he said, clearly resigned.

Sabina turned to Jeremy. "How about you? Are you on board, or does Colonel Johnson stick the Magnum in your face like she did Preston's?"

Jeremy's eyes widened. "She really pulled a gun on you? I thought you were shitting me. Wish I'd been there to see it." His brother grinned wickedly.

Preston stiffened. "It wasn't fucking funny. This shit's serious, and you better start taking it that way."

"It wasn't funny at all," Sabina added quietly. "We're running out of time. If you're not going to admit you're guilty and cooperate, you're getting a one-way ticket to prison."

"I'm not admitting to one damned thing," Jeremy said. "But I'll cooperate since I don't appear to have a choice. The colonel, or anyone else, doesn't have to pull their gun on me."

Preston and Sabina looked at each other, and he could tell she had the same trepidation he did. But, they'd said what they could to convince these two morons. If one or both of them did something stupid, Preston and Sabina would be held responsible, and that pissed him off. Aside from all the mission consequences, if Jeremy fucked this up too, the familial fallout would be irreparable.

They let their brothers shower one at a time. The colonel and the rest of the team returned bearing coffee and arepas. Dominic didn't have much appetite, but Jeremy put away his share of the food and then some.

Then, in detail, the colonel briefed them on their role in the sting and made Jeremy and Dominic rehearse what they were going to do when the representative contacted them. They left to change out of their tactical gear in their hotel room down the hall, leaving Dominic and Jeremy alone.

"I hope to hell they don't fuck up," Preston murmured as the team called up the camera feed to find Dominic sitting, morosely staring into space, and Jeremy pacing.

The colonel raised her eyebrow. "You're not sure of them? I thought you were going to convince them."

"Ma'am, you have no idea what a hard-headed little prick Jeremy is," he told her tiredly.

"Worse than you?" A smile played around her lips.

"I'm not even in his ballpark."

Dominic and Jeremy got the call around noon. Jeremy put the phone on speaker. The representative named the official's price, which was higher than any of their other offers, and said he was on his way to pick up the emeralds. Jeremy immediately went into the spiel he'd rehearsed with the colonel. "We've had cause to reconsider," he said with exactly the right amount of concern. "How do we know you're really with the official? What if you're trying to purchase the emeralds for yourself?"

"I assure you I'm representing him." The guy sounded miffed. "He's made his offer, and you would do well to accept."

"Not until I know for certain I'm dealing with him and not some upstart who's going to get us all killed." Jeremy's voice conveyed the perfect amount of anxiety. "We need to know for certain we're dealing with the official and him alone. We need to pass the stones to him in a face-to-face meeting."

"He never meets with sellers face-to-face," the representative shot back. "You'll deal with me or pay the consequences."

"Or we'll sell the stones elsewhere, and your employer will be out the nicest stones to come out of the mines in a very long time," Jeremy said smoothly. "Those stones will have him sitting pretty for years to come. It seems to me he would be willing to risk a face-to-face meeting to obtain them."

The go-between protested again. "Go back and talk to him," Jeremy insisted. "We need to meet with him ourselves. We want to know who we're selling them to."

"I'll get back to you." The representative clicked off, and Jeremy resumed his pacing.

"Wonder if they'll deal," Sabina asked Colonel Johnson.

"We'll see," the colonel said. "Otherwise, we go to Plan C."

"Surveillance of the go-between?" Eagle asked.

"Won't be easy if we have to go that route," Paco observed quietly.

"Let's hope we don't," Colonel Johnson said. "I don't know about you folks, but I'm ready for something to eat. Jazz, you're in charge of lunch."

Jazz found a street vendor selling empanadas and tamales wrapped in banana leaves. The team munched on the delicious street food and listened in to three more phone calls between Jeremy and the mysterious go-between.

The afternoon crept by. Preston could feel the tension ratcheting up as Colonel Johnson and her team worked on Plan C to follow the representative.

The hoped-for phone call came, and the go-between said stiffly, "My employer's agreed to meet with you in person. But it will be on his terms."

The team gave an enthusiastic thumbs up not shared by Jeremy and Dominic. "What are his terms?" Jeremy asked cautiously.

"He will meet you outside Turbana. You'll be sent exact GPS coordinates once you're on your way with the emeralds. He'll meet you exactly at midnight, not a moment later." The go-between clicked off.

Well, hell. A midnight run, and they didn't even know where they were going. It sounded dangerous and like a set-up.

The team looked at one another with smiles. "Piece of cake," they said.

Preston didn't think so. But then they were the professionals. They should know.

En masse, they trooped down the hall to Jeremy and Dominic's room, where they found Jeremy again pacing and Dominic sitting quietly on the bed, his trembling hands in his lap.

Eagle sat in the chair in front of the desk and pulled up a map of Turbana on his iPad. He looked at the map of the small town with puzzlement. "It's a little place. No parks or anyplace for a midnight meeting I can see."

"Strip center parking lot?" Sabina asked.

"Seems a little public, considering the lengths to which the official's gone to remain anonymous. Anybody could drive up and witness the swap."

"Okay, not a strip center," Sabina said.

"I suppose we'll find out when they send the GPS coordinates," Paco said.

"How will you follow us without being seen?" Jeremy asked.

"Same way we've been doing it for the last week." Colonel Johnson nodded, and Jazz produced three bullet-proof vests. "We secured these yesterday. He may be armed or have bodyguards who are." She handed one each to Dominic and Jeremy and the third to Preston.

Preston examined the vest curiously. It was a military model, but not much different from the one he wore on the job. It should protect him. "Thank you, Colonel."

She dipped her chin.

The colonel sent Sabina for food, and after everyone ate, all they could do was wait as the hours ticked toward zero hundred.

The team was alert, maybe a little buzzed, but nobody seemed nervous or anxious. Paco and Eagle appeared to be reading something on their phones, and Jazz and the colonel had their

AirPods in. Sabina had a new paperback in front of her, and she seemed to be engaged in the story.

The only ones who appeared concerned were Dominic and Jeremy. Preston was too, but he forced himself to remain calm. He had his reader open but couldn't concentrate to save his life. Instead, he kept replaying all the possible ways this could go FUBAR.

They changed back into tactical gear at twenty-two hundred. It was maybe forty-five minutes to Turbana. When Preston asked why they were leaving so early, the colonel told him they were splitting into two groups.

Jazz and Eagle would go on ahead and wait in Turbana. "They can get into place once we have the coordinates," the colonel explained. "We need photographs of the official, not only a visual sighting, and we have to get close enough for them to get a good picture in the dark. Unless this official is well-known, chances are none of us will recognize him, even though we've been looking at the pictures of possible candidates for days. Eagle and Jazz will take the pictures. The rest of us will track Dominic and Jeremy from a few miles back, and we'll be ready to provide protection when it starts to go south."

Shit. She said when, not if.

Jazz and Eagle left, and the three remaining team members sat back down and returned to whatever they were doing to distract themselves. Jeremy and Dominic fidgeted, and Preston wanted to scream. His nerves were stretched razor thin, and he itched to do something. Anything to get this over with and his brother on his way to safety—and, no doubt, incarceration.

It was nearly twenty-three hundred when the colonel signaled Dominic and Jeremy. "Keep your phone line open," she told Dominic. "Jeremy, keep yours on speaker when they call with the coordinates. We'll hear them and follow you." Her expression hardened. "Don't even think of doing one thing off script. You try to ditch us, or do anything stupid, we'll know, and you'll probably get yourselves killed before we can get to you. Got me?" They nodded. "Okay, team. It's showtime."

Paco and Sabina's alert meters ramped up, and she looked *excited*. Preston stared at her in wonder.

She's really looking forward to this.

The whole team was, and they were batshit crazy.

They followed Jeremy and Dominic to the parking garage and gave them a ten-minute head start.

The road to Turbana was deserted, and they were about halfway to the small town when Jeremy's phone rang. A different, heavily accented voice gave them the coordinates. "You'll get more instructions when you arrive," he said and rung off.

Paco entered the coordinates. "It's the cemetery," he said. "You get that, Eagle?"

"Dark and deserted this time of night. Works like a charm," Eagle replied.

Jeremy and Dominic pulled into the cemetery with time to spare. Paco parked a couple of blocks away.

The colonel synced her phone to her earpiece, and they walked silently in the deep shadows through the moonless night and slipped over an iron fence. They went into the cemetery and waited patiently for Jeremy to get more instructions.

The anticipated call came at exactly zero hundred. "Meet us at the *Calderon* monument in the center."

"How—" The voice clicked off before Jeremy could finish his question.

An already less-than-ideal setting became worse. Jeremy and Dominic would have to turn on their phone flashlights, making them easy to track as they made their way through the cemetery.

Then again, so would the team.

They watched from a cautious distance as Jeremy and Dominic haltingly traipsed across the cemetery. Preston's heart pounded as they crept closer. But for their brothers' flashlights, it was pitch black.

Jazz and Eagle must have had a super-zoom light-sensitive camera, or else there was no way they'd get a snap of the official.

Jeremy and Dominic approached what seemed to be the monument. A moment later a large SUV with its lights turned off pulled up and parked behind the stone. An imposing figure stepped out of the vehicle. He seemed to be alone, but in the near absence of light, it was impossible to tell.

"Do you have the emeralds?" the figure asked tersely.

"Are you the official?" Jeremy demanded.

"I am. Now hand over the emeralds."

"Do you have the money?" Jeremy asked.

"I said, hand over the emeralds," the man said harshly.

In response, Jeremy turned his flashlight onto the man's face. Suddenly two more men appeared at the man's side, both brandishing weapons. They trained their weapons on Jeremy and Dominic.

"The emeralds," the man snarled.

Jeremy's hands shook as he handed over the bag containing the stones. There was a moment of silence, then the man spoke.

"Shoot them. No witnesses." He turned to go back to his car.

Shots rang out in the night, and the two men on either side of the official fell. The official reached for Dominic, but Jeremy pushed Dominic to one side and launched himself at the official.

Three more men appeared out of the darkness. One leaned over and shot Dominic directly in the chest as the other two grabbed Jeremy by the arms and dragged him away with the official on their heels. The colonel and her team ran toward the fleeing official, but he leaped into the SUV, and he and his men were out of the cemetery before they could be stopped.

"Damn, damn, damn," Paco said quietly as they walked back to where Dominic lay on the ground groaning. "The bastards got away."

"I got a facial match," Eagle said. "It's Senator Raimondo Valenzuela. Which is to be expected. Typical political hypocrite.

He's been spearheading the fight for law and order, and to clean up Colombian corruption."

Preston looked at them disbelievingly. "Why are we standing here talking about the senator and not going after them? Hurry. We have to get to the car if we're going to catch up," Preston nearly shouted as Sabina helped her brother off the ground.

Preston looked at the team standing by the monument. "What the fuck are you waiting for? We have to catch them. They have Jeremy!"

They all turned to look at him. "We've achieved our objective," the colonel said quietly. "We have a clear picture of the senator to turn over to the State Department."

"What about Jeremy?" Preston demanded.

"I need to get my team home safely," Colonel Johnson said.

He stared at her in horror. "You don't mean that," he breathed. "You *can't* mean it. We have to do something. They'll kill Jeremy."

Preston looked around at the solemn faces surrounding him. "No, please. Don't do this to him." He turned to Sabina, cursing the tears filling his eyes. "Please. He's my brother. The only brother I have. Don't make me go home and tell my mother her baby's gone."

Tears poured out of his eyes and ran down his cheeks.

"Please."

Chapter Fourteen
Sabina

Sabina flinched at Preston's stark sorrow. She looked over at Dominic. Her brother was wheezing and clutching the front of the bullet-proof vest. He probably had several broken ribs, but he was alive and well. He was here and not in the SUV because Jeremy had pushed him to one side. Thanks to Preston's brother, she wouldn't have the unthinkable job of telling her family her only brother was dead.

Unlike Preston.

She bit her lip as she took in a man who sobbed like a child. Her heart broke for him.

This wasn't right.

"Colonel, permission to speak freely," Sabina said.

The colonel turned to her. "Go ahead."

"I think we ought to at least try to save Mr. Ramos's brother."

"And why would that be?" Colonel Johnson looked at her. "Why should I risk my team for a known criminal? I'm tasked with getting my team home safely. As bad as I feel about Jeremy Ramos, your lives take priority."

"He made sure you got the pictures you needed. If he'd acted according to plan, he wouldn't have shined the flashlight in the senator's face, and the exchange would've gone off as planned. He and Dominic would've had a chance to get to safety.

"Instead, he deliberately aimed his flashlight at the senator's face long enough for Eagle to get a good picture. If he hadn't, I doubt that the pictures would've been good enough to make an identification.

We owe him a rescue for that, if no other reason." Sabina took a deep breath. "He saved my brother. They would've snatched Dominic if Jeremy hadn't pushed him out of the way. I don't have to go home and tell Mom her baby's dead. It's not right Preston has to."

"She's right." Dominic stood as straight as he could and looked the colonel in the eye. "We talked about it on the way here. You were going to do all you could to protect us, so we'd make sure there was enough light to get a decent picture. Was that a mistake on our part? Should we have let you take your chances with the picture?" He looked around at the team. "Tell her. Whichever of you took the pictures. Tell her it made a difference."

"Did it?" the colonel asked quietly.

"Yeah, it made a difference," Eagle admitted. "It made a huge difference. Now, even after having a darkened photo cleaned up, it wouldn't hold up as well as the one we got."

The colonel looked around at the team with a question in her eyes. Slowly, reluctantly, one by one they nodded. "Okay, then. We can try. Does he still have the tracker on him?"

Sabina got out her phone. "No. It's in their car."

Paco ran off a series of numbers and letters. "That's the license plate. I caught a glimpse of it as they drove away."

"That's a start," Colonel Johnson said. "We'll go back to the hotel and find out who the car's registered to and what address or addresses are involved, then go from there." She turned to Preston. "It's probably going to take us some time to track him down. We'll work as fast as we can, but we have no guarantees we'll get there in time to save him."

Preston wiped the tears from his cheeks. "But you're going to try, and I know you guys. You're not big on failure. So, thank you." He looked around the group. "Thanks to all of you for being willing to stick your necks out for him. I know what you said, Colonel. But I'd bet my next year's salary he's coming home with us."

"'Preciate the vote of confidence." The colonel gave him a small smile. "Okay, team. We reconvene at zero six hundred. By then Paco and Eagle should have the owner of the car's address, as well as the senator's address. We go from there. Mr. Kaslov, when we get back to the hotel, I'll want to examine your chest and abdomen for injuries." Dominic nodded.

Preston was silent on the drive back to Cartagena. Paco and Eagle took off so Eagle could hack the Colombian vehicle registry and track the plate. Sabina followed Colonel Johnson and Dominic back to his room. His chest was covered with blooming purple bruises, and Colonel Johnson diagnosed three broken ribs. "I can tape them if you think it will help."

"Nah. I'll be fine." Dominic's face clouded. "I hope Jeremy makes it."

"So do I," Sabina said quietly.

She left Dominic and found Preston talking quietly with Jazz in their room. "You have a place to sleep tonight?" she asked Jazz.

"The colonel wants me to stay with Dominic." Jazz looked at her and shrugged.

"Surely she doesn't think he's going to run away in his condition," Sabina said tiredly.

"No, but if he starts coughing or puking up blood, she wants somebody there to take care of him. She's still a nurse at heart." Jazz wished them a good evening and left.

Preston sank down on the bed and put his head in his hands. "Do you think the team can get to him in time?" he mumbled.

"I hope we can. We'll give it our best shot." She sat down beside him and put her arm around his waist. "We'll be as committed as we are on all our other missions."

They sat quietly. "Why was this mission so critical?" he asked. "Why does our government care so much about the identity of a corrupt Colombian official?"

Sabina paused, then let out a long sigh. "What the fuck. You know everything else." She drew in a deep breath. "The senator has ties to a terrorist organization operating throughout Central America and Mexico. They also have cells in some of our southern states. The money he's making from the illegal emerald trade is being channeled into those cells on American soil."

"What the fuck?"

"The government wouldn't've sent us down there if there weren't implications to our country."

Preston shook his head. "Why'd you stick out your neck for Jeremy?" he asked. "You don't like him. Or me. He's a thief and a criminal. You blame him for involving Dominic, and you're right. But you still persuaded the colonel and the team to try to save him. Why?"

"For the reasons I gave her."

He nodded. "But there was more. Wasn't there?"

She didn't want to have this or any conversation regarding family ties, but they'd been through too much together not to tell him the truth.

"There was," she admitted. "Yeah, Jeremy's dishonorable, but so is Dominic. Yet, I love him with all my heart. The same way you love Jeremy. I know all about loving a criminal brother. Regardless, I would hate to lose my brother, and I'd hate for you to lose yours."

He leaned over and kissed her on the temple. "Thanks. Really. It means a lot."

***

Sabina's heart fell as Paco and Eagle came out of the abandoned house. "Another dead end," Paco said to the waiting team. "If they were here earlier, they're gone now."

Preston wilted at her side. "Do we have any other leads?" he asked defeatedly to no one in particular. "Or was this the last possibility?"

"We have a few more," Colonel Johnson said. "But only a few."

Preston's shoulders sagged as they trooped to their vehicles.

The gray light of early dawn illuminated their tired faces. For the third night in a row, they'd been out all night.

It'd been three days since the senator and his henchmen had spirited Jeremy away, and the team was beginning to lose hope of ever tracking him down.

Sabina was trying to remain optimistic for Preston's sake, but as lead after lead fizzled out, it was getting harder and harder to hide her discouragement.

It would soon be time to get on a plane and go home, Jeremy or no Jeremy.

At first it had seemed promising. By the next morning, Paco and Eagle had learned the SUV was registered to one Guillermo Aldape of Sabanalarga, a small town about an hour and a half outside Cartagena.

Interestingly, Aldape wasn't a known associate of the senator's, but he did have known ties to a couple of *guaqueros*, neither of whom seemed to have any ties to *El Lobo*.

Further searching had revealed Aldape's ties to a once-active rebel group that was thought to've gone dormant in the early two thousands. But night raids on Aldape's home and the most recent addresses of the *guaqueros* had turned up nothing. Visits to the rebel group leaders' homes also came up empty.

A midnight visit to the senator's home had produced an address book with several sets of initials and phone numbers, but the numbers had traced back to burner phones and were no help.

The clock was ticking. Jeremy had been in their hands for three days, and if the team didn't find him in the next day or two, there might be nothing to find. A dead body to take home to the Ramos family might be the only outcome of this seemingly doomed mission.

The team was silent as they drove back to Cartagena. They'd moved out of their hotel rooms in the dead of night and were staying in a safe house in a nondescript neighborhood on the outskirts of town.

Preston and Sabina had moved into a room together. The colonel had offered to share with her, but she'd chosen to stay with Preston, despite the raised eyebrows and questioning looks she'd gotten from other team members.

She knew her time with Preston was running out. It was highly unlikely they'd see each other once they were back home.

Their relationship was a moment out of time, not something they would continue once they were back to their lives in the real world. So, she was determined to have what little time left she had with him.

Now, the colonel outlined their plans for the next night: they'd check out the last four addresses they had. Then she told them all to get some rest.

Sabina followed Preston down the hall and into their room. She put her weapons and burglary tools away while he hit the shower. She stripped and followed him in the en-suite bathroom, where she found him standing under a hot spray aimed at his back and shoulders.

His face was drawn, and for the first time since she'd met him, he looked older than his thirty-eight years.

"It's not looking good," he said defeatedly as she climbed into the shower beside him.

"As long as we have places to check, we have hope," she told him. She poured bath gel on a washcloth and ran it down Preston's back. "I'm not giving up until we check out the last place on the list. And you shouldn't either."

"I'm trying, but it's hard. Have you heard from Dominic?"

"No. But Colonel Bustamante contacted Colonel Johnson and said that he got home and is in protective custody at the hospital until we get back and can be debriefed. When it all comes out, I imagine he'll be charged and arraigned without a bail recommendation, and his lawyer and the DOJ will work out whatever deal his lawyer can persuade them to take. Then he'll go to prison." She dropped her head to his back. "My parents are going to be beside themselves when they find out."

"Right now, I'd give my right nut to have my brother in the feds' protective custody." He turned around and ran his hands down Sabina's wet body. "Are you here only for the shower?"

"I'm here for all kinds of reasons. Some involve water over naked bodies and that right nut of yours." She gripped his already hard cock and caressed his balls. "Reasons like this."

"Good reasons." He smiled crookedly.

"Yeah." She edged him over enough to stand under the spray full-on. "Too bad we're not in one of those fancy places with multiple showerheads."

"We'll make do." He moved so their bodies were stuck together, her breasts digging into his chest and his cock pressing into her lower stomach. "How's this?"

"Really good. Kiss me, Preston."

She tilted her face up, and he lowered his. Their lips met in a soft press that slowly turned wet and deep. The kiss communicated all the caring that was unspoken yet very real. They clung together for long moments, letting their lips, tongues, and mouths express their feelings.

Sabina touched and stroked his muscled waist and his rock-hard butt, his cock pressing harder into her as she explored him.

His hands were equally busy, stroking tenderly, lovingly, making her heart pound and her nipples pebble.

Heat pooled between her legs, her dampness mingling with the body gel and the water on Preston's skilled fingers.

By now he knew what she liked and how to caress her so that she would come apart at his touch. She opened for him to let him do his magic, her body tightening with anticipation until it exploded in a kaleidoscope of pleasure.

She tipped her head back, his name on her lips as she came in his arms.

Her legs trembled as he turned her around and used the body gel on her back and shoulders. She picked up the shampoo and squirted some in his hair and then hers. They soaped their hair and again stood together under the spray as the water beat down on their heads, carrying the suds from their bodies.

She looked down at his swollen cock. "Are we going for full-on shower sex?" she asked with a smile.

He looked down at her with a wicked grin. "Absolutely."

He hoisted her up, and without another word, he entered her with a single thrust. They began to move, slowly at first and then harder and faster as they seemed to pour everything they felt for one another into this joining. This was more than great sex. This was all she felt but could not, would not, say out loud. It was the caring and compassion, the tenderness she felt for this most unlikely of men.

This was everything she hadn't wanted to feel but felt for him anyway.

Love, she admitted. Love she hadn't wanted, in a relationship that could go nowhere.

Sabina's body began to spiral out of control, her back arching, and she gave a shout of release as another hard climax surged through her.

Preston followed with a single thrust as his cock trembled inside her throbbing body. As she felt the jets of his release, she realized they'd forgotten to use a condom. She had a clean bill of health, and she was on birth control.

Now that she knew Preston, she doubted he slept around or had been careless with other women.

He eased himself out of her body and held her until her feet were flat on the shower floor. He looked down at his unsheathed cock.

"I don't think we have anything to worry about. I'm on birth control," she assured him.

"I've got no worries." He grinned, turned off the water, and reached for the towels. "I've never forgotten protection until tonight," he told her.

"You're distracted and worried." She put her arms around him. "I forgot too." She toweled the moisture off her chest and legs. "It'll be a while 'til sunset. You want to see what we can find to eat before we have another go?" She wasn't about to say it out loud, but it would beat lying awake and worrying. Which was what Preston would do if they went to bed now.

Besides, they didn't have much longer together, and she wanted to build as many beautiful memories as she could.

Preston nodded. They yanked on sweatpants and tees and raided the refrigerator for the last of the tres leches, which didn't taste all that different from the San Antonio variety. By the time they'd finished their cake, Preston's cock was at half-mast again, and Sabina took it as a sign.

They came together again, and this time they went slow. Every touch deliberate, every kiss tender, every caress an expression of the unspoken bond between them.

He left no part of her body untouched, his fingers and lips setting her on fire. She touched him too, her fingers stroking his rigid cock until it was rock-hard.

When they couldn't wait any longer, he opened her legs and pushed his way inside, his cock slipping into her.

They began to move together, slowly at first, then faster in a sensual ballet that had her spiraling out of control. When she let go, he went with her, giving her one last powerful thrust that had her gasping as he came apart in her arms.

They held on to one another as the high slowly faded. Preston withdrew from her body and rolled to lie beside her.

Sabina snuggled into him and wondered what he would do if she told him she loved him. She supposed it would be easier and less painful if the words remained unspoken.

As it was, walking away from him was going to be one of the hardest things she'd ever done.

Chapter Fifteen

Sabina

Sabina and the team assembled in the small living room promptly at nineteen hundred. "We have three more possibilities to check this evening," Colonel Johnson told them. "Two are in Baranoa, and one is outside Campo de la Cruz. They belong to relatives of the *guaqueros* and are thought to have basements where a captive could be concealed."

"And if he's not in any of those places?" Preston asked quietly.

"I don't have an answer for you right now." Colonel Johnson looked at him with compassion when she said, "We can do more electronic searching to see if we turn up anything."

Preston nodded. The sun was setting as they made their way out of Cartagena and down the highway for the two-hour drive to Baranoa. They were mostly silent on the way.

Preston appeared to be lost in thought, and Jazz and Colonel Johnson were watching the road.

Sabina wondered if Preston had given any thought as to what he was going to say to his parents if they couldn't find Jeremy. His father would probably raise hell: excoriate Preston and threaten the Army. Not that it would help or change things. They'd already gone above and beyond trying to save a criminal who'd committed major crimes in the U.S. and in a foreign country. Not that the elder Ramos would see it that way.

It'd been dark for a while when they reached Baranoa, a good-sized town that was big enough that there were businesses still open and traffic still clogged the streets.

The colonel entered the first address on their list into the GPS, and they found themselves in a wealthy enclave with rock fences surrounding the houses, some of which were bound to have private guards.

"Hmm. So much for slipping in and out with no issues," Jazz said.

"But the flip side is that a house like this, with a wall and guards, is more likely to be where Jeremy's being held than a cracker box with no safeguards," Sabina said.

Colonel Johnson fiddled with her GPS. "There's a municipal park a half mile from here. Paco and Eagle can meet us there. We'll find out what we can and come up with a plan."

Paco had found the house's plans by the time they rendezvoused in the park. They looked at the diagrams of the first and second floor. "There's no basement on here," Paco said. "But if you look closely, there appears to be stairs off the kitchen leading down. I'd put money it's a basement of some kind."

"Probably," Jazz agreed. "The question is, who's there, and how much protection are we going to be plowing through?"

"Jazz, Eagle, you two need to do a quick recon of the place," Colonel Johnson said. "Go over the wall. See if there are guards or dogs. If you can, look in the windows and see if you can spot anyone else. We'll wait here, and Paco can do a little more electronic searching."

Jazz and Eagle vanished into the night. Paco turned to his electronics. "It belongs to Juan Rios's brother-in-law, who's one of Aldape's *guaqueros*. The brother-in-law is also believed to be into emerald smuggling. According to the tax rolls, Rios lives there with his wife and mother-in-law."

"Three people in that huge place makes sense. We've gotten a load of how profitable illegal emeralds are," Sabina said.

"That is, if you can stay alive long enough to enjoy them," Preston stated.

Jazz and Eagle reappeared in about half an hour. "Two guards roaming the grounds. We can take them out, no problem," Jazz said. "No dogs."

"What about inside?" the colonel asked.

"Whoever's in there is upstairs," Eagle said. "If Jeremy's being held in the basement, it's possible we could get in and out without being detected. If not, we neutralize." He looked at the colonel. "Temporary or permanent?"

"Temporary if we can. Permanent if we have to."

The team slipped through the shadows to the house. It was a beautiful old home, white with imposing columns across the entire front. A six-foot-tall brick fence with an iron railing on top surrounded it, and massive iron gates guarded the driveway.

Sabina's lip curled as she climbed over the fence. Under other circumstances she would've admired the house and the good taste of the owners in choosing it. But this house was purchased with dirty money, and she was less than impressed.

They scaled the wall with no problem. They kept to the shadows as they crept between the massive trees, where a bored-looking guard stood, smoking a cigarette on the front sidewalk. The colonel nodded to Eagle, and he slipped up behind the guard and jabbed him in the neck with a syringe full of heavy-duty sedative. The guard collapsed into Eagle's arms, and he lowered the guy to the ground.

"One down, one to go," Colonel Johnson murmured.

They slipped around the house, prepared to neutralize the second guard, but he was not at his expected post at the back door. A quick search didn't locate the man, and they were about to take their chances and go ahead when he came out the back door. He turned around when someone called out from inside.

"*Sí, señora. Callaré al norteamericano.*" He turned around and went back in the house. *Yes, ma'am. I will silence the North American.*

They looked at one another. The *norteamericano* was most likely Jeremy.

If he needed silencing, he was still alive.

Sabina felt hope bloom anew in her chest. Maybe Preston could take his little brother home after all.

They gave the guard a minute to get back in the house. Paco got two more injections ready—one for the guard and another for whomever he was talking to. They went into the house and found themselves in a recently renovated kitchen. The woman the guard had been talking to must've gone upstairs. The door to the stairs was open, and they could hear moaning coming from the basement.

They all looked at one another. It had to be Jeremy.

They started toward the stairs, single file. They heard another moan and a harsh "*Cállate, norteamericano,*" and the sound of a blow followed by a scream of pain, then repeated blows and more groaning.

They picked up the pace. Guns drawn, they abandoned all attempts at stealth and ran down the stairs, where they found the guard holding a metal pipe and standing over a bloody figure tied to a chair.

Preston stared in unadulterated horror at the figure that was at first unrecognizable, but on a second examination was the beaten, tortured body of Jeremy Ramos. Most likely tortured for whatever information they thought he could share with them, and they probably got off on inflicting pain.

The team fanned out and surrounded the guard, who looked at them defiantly. "Shoot me and everyone upstairs will hear you," he said contemptuously in heavily accented English.

"Not a problem. We'll kill them too." The colonel looked over at Jeremy, and her expression hardened.

Sabina had seen a lot in her career of the ugliness one human could inflict on another, but what they had put Jeremy through was right up there at the top.

His naked body was covered with whip marks and blistering burns, and both legs appeared to be broken. His once-handsome face was sliced to bits, and she doubted that even the most skilled surgeons would ever have him looking like he once had.

His chest and abdomen were a mass of bruises, the kind that spoke of internal injuries. Jeremy's head sagged, and he appeared to be unconscious, probably rendered so from the blows they'd heard coming down the stairs.

"Shit, cut him out of the chair and find something to use as a stretcher," Colonel Johnson instructed. "We're going to have to carry him to the car." Sabina moved to Jeremy's side.

"You're not taking him anywhere," the guard spat.

"You have to be fucking kidding me," Eagle said. "You've got five guns trained on you, asshole."

The guard raised his gun, and all five of their pistols spat in unison. He fell to the floor. "You...you." His head lolled to one side, and he sucked in his last breath.

Preston walked over and kicked his body. "That was too damned merciful. I wish I could've spent an hour or two working on him."

"Easy, Mr. Ramos," the colonel soothed. She turned to Sabina. "Go find a blanket or a quilt. Shoot anybody who tries to stop you. These assholes have earned permanent neutralization."

Sabina moved up the stairs. Her best bet was a blanket or quilt from a bed, so she ran up a second flight of stairs and ducked into the first bedroom she came to. There was a promising-looking comforter on the bed, and she was in the process of yanking it off when an imperious-looking middle-aged woman stomped into the room, stopping only when she realized Sabina's gun was pointed at her. "What are you doing in my house?" she demanded sharply. "Did you get lost or something?" If she was afraid, it didn't show.

"Are you the bitch who wanted the *norteamericano* silenced?" Sabina asked conversationally.

"I was." She looked down her nose at Sabina. "He was disturbing my reading."

Sabina shot her between the eyes. "That's better."

She did a quick search of the upstairs rooms, but there didn't appear to be anyone else up here. She ran down the stairs with the comforter. "Will this work?"

The colonel nodded. "It'll do."

Sabina and Jazz spread the comforter on the floor, and as gently as they could, Eagle and Paco laid the nearly lifeless Jeremy in the middle. Each of the men picked up a corner, and they were halfway up the stairs when they heard a car barreling down the driveway.

"Fuck. It's about to turn into a shitshow," Colonel Johnson said.

The men ran up the stairs with Jeremy and laid him underneath the kitchen table. They took up defensive positions at each door to the kitchen: Paco and Colonel Johnson went to the back door; Sabina and Preston were positioned at the door to the dining room, with Eagle and Jazz at the door to the laundry. They waited behind the doors and listened as the car pulled into the garage. They could hear at least three men's voices coming, all sounding worried. "Aldape said the North Americans were snooping around his cousin's house last night. They better not come here. We'll blow them away."

Sabina smiled to herself. *You go on thinking that.*

"They're getting too close," another voice said. "We need to work on the *pendejo* in the basement a little more. He's bound to crack sooner or later."

A third voice chimed in. "If he knew anything the senator would be interested in, he would have already told us. We need to kill him."

"No, we'll give it one more try." The door into the laundry room opened, and three men strode into the kitchen, then stopped in their tracks when they spotted five guns trained on them. One of them pushed a button on his phone, but at that point, a rain of bullets felled the three where they stood.

"We need to get out of here." The colonel nudged one of the dead bodies with her foot. "He punched something on his phone. He was calling in the cavalry."

They didn't need to be told twice. They dragged Jeremy out from under the table and carried him out the back door. They ran out the open gates and were halfway to the park when they all heard chopper blades. "What the fuck," Sabina breathed. "They called in a helicopter search?"

"Shit. It's either mercenaries or the senator has the military in his pocket. Into the shadows, everybody," Colonel Johnson ordered.

They ducked into the shadows of another estate and hunkered down under some trees. Sabina's heart pounded as she watched the helicopter move in a searching pattern.

The chopper circled for a good fifteen minutes before moving to the other side of the neighborhood. Sticking to the shadows as much as they were able, they made their way back to the cars. A quick check confirmed that the vehicles were still in working order and didn't have tracking devices on them.

"We're splitting up, and we're not taking the main highway." The colonel indicated two smaller roads out of town. "Paco, you take this one, and Jazz can take the other. Lay Jeremy on my back seat." She turned to Preston. "I'm the only medic on this mission, and I want him near me." Preston nodded. She rattled off coordinates. "We'll rendezvous at this point. I've already sent for a plane with medical facilities."

"Thank you, everyone," Preston said quietly into the dark.

They climbed into their respective vehicles, and Jazz and the colonel went first. Preston watched with hooded eyes as the other car, without benefit of headlights, made its way out of the park and onto a side street. "He's torn up bad. Real bad." He turned to Sabina. "Do you think he'll make it?"

"Depends on the extent of his internal injuries. What was done to him was more to inflict pain to get him to talk than it was to injure or kill him."

"He's going to be scarred. His face. He used to be so handsome."

"A good surgeon can do wonders," Eagle said quietly from the front seat.

"What about the crap we left in the safe house?" Preston asked.

"It's already been taken care of," Sabina told him. "By the same source who supplied us the house."

As to who that source was and what their arrangement was with the Army, she didn't know and didn't care.

The four of them fell silent. Exhaustion swamped Sabina, but she was too tense to sleep. A part of her half expected the chopper to follow them down the road, and she didn't relax until they'd pulled off the highway and bounced down a rutted dirt path to where a small Learjet waited.

The other team members' car was already parked by the runway beside a rundown pickup truck. The four of them wasted no time getting on the plane, where they found Jeremy already strapped to a stretcher with an IV running into his arm. Colonel Johnson was sitting in a seat next to Jeremy, and Jazz was sprawled in a seat in the back, snoring softly.

Paco and Eagle took the two seats closest to the front, leaving two near the stretcher for Sabina and Preston. They barely had their seatbelts on when the plane's engines fired up and they taxied into position. Sabina leaned her head back against the headrest, exhaustion and relief swamping her as the little jet accelerated for takeoff.

Jeremy moaned, and the colonel moved over him. "How is he?" Preston asked softly. "He doesn't look good." The lights illuminating the stretcher revealed every injury in gory detail, at least those not covered by the warming blanket loosely thrown over Jeremy.

"He's holding his own," Colonel Johnson said cautiously. "We'll know more when we get him to the hospital and the trauma docs can examine him." She turned to Preston. "We got him out alive, which is a miracle in and of itself. To be honest, Mr. Ramos, I had little hope we'd find him alive, if at all." She smiled faintly. "This is one of those times I'm glad to be wrong."

"Thank you," Preston said solemnly. "I'll never be able to thank you enough."

The plane was in the air and leveling off when Preston asked Sabina, "What kind of future can he expect if he does make it?"

"He'll be treated for his injuries, he'll get better, and then he'll have to answer for what he did," Sabina answered. "He and Dominic both. I wish I could tell you differently."

"I wish you could too. Does your family know what's happened?"

"If I had to guess, no. They're going to be upset and angry when they find out what's been going on, and they're going to be really unhappy when they find out I was involved. They'll expect me to get him out of trouble, and I can't."

"Can't or won't?"

"Can't. Every member of the team knows what happened. I'd look like an idiot if I tried." Her lips trembled. "But I wouldn't even if I could." She turned to Preston, cursing the tears in her eyes. "It's killing me knowing he's going to prison for who knows how long. But either I'm honest or I'm not."

She wiped her face with her sleeve. "And you have to do the same."

Chapter Sixteen

Preston

Preston glanced at Sabina, who was leaning against the window, sound asleep. He'd shoved a jacket under her head when she'd first nodded off, and she hadn't budged since. She was exhausted. They all were. And she'd been wired all the way from Baranoa until the plane lifted off.

Now that she knew she was safe and on her way home, she could rest, even knowing what she had to face when she got there. Her family was going to be pissed as all get-out if she didn't do everything in her power to get her brother out of trouble.

Not because they were Romani but because they were parents who loved their son and would expect his sister to do what she could to cover his ass. As Preston's parents were going to expect him to do.

Which left him with a dilemma.

He'd gone on this mission to protect Jeremy's best interests. As far as he was concerned, he'd done that. Otherwise, the team would've left his brother to his fate. But his father was going to expect him to do more and wasn't going to take no for an answer.

Except Preston couldn't do more.

He was dropping off to sleep when his brother began thrashing around restlessly. Colonel Johnson took Jeremy's vitals and spoke soothingly, but his brother continued to move about. Colonel Johnson looked over at Preston. "He needs to settle down, or he's going to injure himself even more. Think you can calm him?"

"I can try."

They switched places. Preston reached for Jeremy's hand but realized some of his fingers were broken, and all of the fingernails had been pulled out. Instead, he leaned over his brother, trying to disguise his horror at Jeremy's damaged face.

"Jeremy, it's me." He made his voice as soothing as he could. "Chill, little brother. You're safe."

He repeated his assurances over and over. At first it seemed to have no effect, but slowly Jeremy calmed down and the thrashing stopped. Finally, he opened his eyes a slit. "I'm dreaming," Jeremy murmured. "Or I'm dead."

Preston felt his small smile bloom. "You're not dreaming, and you're not dead. We found you. You're on a plane heading home."

"I'm not dead," Jeremy murmured. "I hurt too much to be dead."

Preston turned to Colonel Johnson. "Can he have anything for the pain?"

"I've already given him as much as I can safely administer," Colonel Johnson said softly. "Maybe in a couple of hours."

"Thank you." He turned back to Jeremy. "We can't give you any more right now, Jer."

His brother mumbled something that sounded like "shit," shut his eyes for a minute, and opened them again. "I'm fucked, aren't I?"

Pretty much. "No, you're not fucked. It may take a while, but you'll recover."

"And then what?"

"I don't know." Preston hoped Jeremy couldn't hear the lie.

"Don't lie to me. I'm in deep shit."

Preston didn't know what to say. He owed Jeremy the truth, but right now his brother's life hung in the balance, and Jeremy needed to fight. If he realized how bleak his future was, he might not be willing to put up the fight that would save him.

"How about you don't worry about it right now. We'll work on getting you better and worry about all that later."

"Hard not to. Damn." His brother shifted and winced. "I was going to be sitting pretty for the rest of my life. Me and Dominic.

We'd have had the ten million and the killing we would have made on the emeralds." He looked up at Preston. "Is Dominic all right, or did they kill him?"

"He's fine. Took a couple of bullets in the vest. He's back at home."

"Probably singing like a bird." Jeremy wheezed. "I wouldn't trust him as far as I can throw him."

"But you saved him."

"I love the SOB. He thinks I'm a good booty call."

Wonderful.

Preston sighed. Maybe he shouldn't say anything, but the question burned. "Why? You're Dad's heir apparent. He paid you a shit-ton, and in a few years, you would've taken the whole thing over. You'd have been plenty rich. So why?"

Jeremy was silent for so long that Preston thought he wasn't going to answer. "Because I could," he whispered finally. "Because I damn well could."

He shut his eyes and said no more.

Preston stared down at his brother's ruined face and thought, *What an asshole.*

Jeremy settled and appeared to be sleeping. Preston laid his head back and let exhaustion overtake him. He wasn't conscious again until he felt the bump as the plane touched down.

The sun was shining brightly on the runway. He could tell from what little he saw out the window that this was no pasture where they were landing. The runway was lined with hangars and other military buildings.

"We had to land at Kelly," Sabina said to his unasked question.

"We couldn't get an ambulance to any of our usual landing places," Colonel Johnson added. She looked at Jeremy, who appeared to be sleeping. "I gave him something for the pain a couple of hours ago. He should sleep through the transfer."

"Where will he be taken? I'll need to inform my family."

"SAMMC, on base," Colonel Johnson said.

Preston wasn't surprised. Not only did the big San Antonio Army hospital have the best trauma department in the city, it would probably be easier to keep his brother in protective custody there until the legal process could start.

The team gathered their duffles and equipment and vacated the plane. Preston waited until the Army medics had loaded his brother into the Army ambulance and whisked him away. The rest of the team had disappeared except for Sabina.

"Do you need a ride home?" she asked.

"I do. But isn't your car out in a pasture somewhere?"

She pointed her thumb to where it was parked waiting for her. "Gotcha."

They didn't say anything on their way back to his house. He gathered up his duffle, which miraculously had been waiting for him on the plane, and gave her a questioning look. "I have a feeling this isn't over. I'll be seeing you again."

She nodded. "It's far from over. And yes, our paths are going to cross again. There'll be debriefings and more debriefings, and, at some point, our brothers will have to stand trial. We may be giving testimony for months, if not years. Such a fun thing to look forward to."

"Not really." He glanced at his front door. "I need to update my father on what went down in Colombia." She opened her mouth, and he held up his hand. "I know, I know. I'm not going to say anything about the mission. Only what happened to Jeremy. Something else I'm not looking forward to."

"Same here. See you."

No kiss goodbye, nothing to indicate they meant anything to each other. She backed out of his driveway and was gone.

Preston unlocked his front door with the key he'd taped to the underside of the passenger chair in her car. He stepped inside and coughed at the musty smell from weeks of disuse.

He got a beer out of the fridge and plopped down on the sofa.

He knew he had to call his father and tell him they were home. But he would finish his beer first, take a shower, put on clean clothes, and then decide what the fuck he was going to tell his father.

Sitting on the sofa in his clean clothes, he sipped a second beer and let his thoughts drift to Sabina, wondering if the conversation with her family would be as contentious as the upcoming discussion with his.

He wished he could talk to her about it tomorrow or the next day, but he didn't think she'd want to. Apparently, for her, it was over.

She'd said nothing about continuing their relationship, and neither had he. It seemed they'd concluded their liaison, or affair, or whatever the fuck it'd been, and it was now a thing of the past.

He sighed. Going in, they'd both known their nights together were an interlude out of time with a definite expiration date. He'd thought it would be enough. He'd thought he'd be able to walk away from her and what they had, then go back to his life with no regrets.

He'd thought she would be nothing more than a memory in what had been an otherwise harrowing experience.

He'd thought way fuckin' wrong.

***

Preston's father folded his arms and looked across his desk to where Preston stood. "So you're telling me you believe Jeremy was actually cooperating with this Dominic Kaslov the whole time and wasn't down there against his will?"

Preston resisted the urge to roll his eyes. "On some level you knew it, or you wouldn't've insisted I go with them to protect his interests. Believe me, he more than cooperated. He was an active participant."

"How do you know? Are you taking the word of that woman and the team she works with?" his father scoffed. "I would've thought better of you than that."

"Such a ringing endorsement. They bugged his room. I saw and heard it all. I listened to him make plans with Dominic. I listened to him offer the stolen gems to six different buyers. I watched him break into a house and steal the damned things. I watched him naked in bed with Dominic until Sabina turned off the feed.

"If that wasn't enough, he admitted to me that he, not his lover, was behind stealing the money from the company. I didn't take anybody's word for anything. I saw and heard him do every damned bit of it.

"Take off your fucking rose-colored glasses and have a good look at your precious baby. He's no victim. He's an international criminal. He's guilty of breaking the law here and in Colombia. And, Dad, Jeremy owes the family's company ten million dollars."

"There...there must have been a good reason," his father blustered. "He never would've been so disloyal to the company otherwise."

"I asked what his reason was. He said because he damned well could." Preston rubbed his hand over his tired eyes. "Face it, Dad. Your little darling's as guilty as sin."

"My little darling's damned near death, that's what he is. Even if he is guilty of the things you say, you didn't protect him like you were supposed to do."

"Fine. I get it. You don't care what he's done. Never mind the shit he's pulled. It's all about Jeremy."

His father looked baffled. "Of course it's all about Jeremy. Why should I care what he's done? I could give a rat's ass if Jeremy's guilty. It's not about any of that. It's about my boy not sitting in a damned federal prison for years of his life. He's already paid a high price for what he's done. Did you get a good look at him? He's never going to be the same. So yes, I'm going to protect my son. I need him to take over this company, because you won't man up and do it yourself. And you need to get on board with protecting him."

"So it's all my fault."

"You let him get hurt. Those damned soldiers didn't do a thing to help him. You should've stepped in and stopped him. I don't give a shit what that colonel told you."

"So it would've been all right with you if I'd defied the colonel and she'd shot me dead, so long as Jeremy was protected. Glad to know where I stand."

"I told you to fuck that little sergeant. She would've saved you."

"I *did* fuck her." Preston felt a sense of disloyalty to Sabina as he said the words. *She was more than a fuck to you, and you know it.*

He swung round to face his father. "She still would've stood there while the colonel blew me away. And that team you're so quick to denigrate could've flown back four days ago and left Jeremy to his fate. But the sergeant stuck her neck out and told the colonel to go back to try to save him. So before you start trash-mouthing Sabina or her team, you need to think about that."

Preston was disgusted with himself for putting up with this shit. "You know what? To hell with this. You'd be willing to see me dead, so long as your spoiled brat's saved. Never mind thanking me for losing another three weeks' pay and saving his thieving ass. I promised myself I'd done all I was going to do for the little fucker, and I meant it."

He marched toward the door to his father's office.

"You walk out that door and we're done. I'm at the end of my rope with you."

"You're at the end of your rope? Great. So am I. You don't give a shit about me anyway." Preston turned around and started to walk away.

"Damn it, Preston, don't do this. I don't feel like that, and you know it."

Preston turned around slowly. "Really? You told me you were fine sacrificing me for Jeremy. And this wasn't the first time, but hear this, it's the last."

"All right. I'm sorry. You're right. You had no choice but to do what the colonel told you. I get it. The outcome is the best you could manage under the circumstances. Now sit down. We need to talk about damage control."

"Damage control? There's no controlling this."

"Yes, damage control. What we can do at this point to salvage the mess Jeremy's landed our family in. Please, Preston. Listen to me a minute." Preston was one foot out the door when his father pulled out his ace. "Please. For your family."

Preston stopped. "Damage control. For the family."

"Yes, damage control, and of course it's for the family."

Preston shook his head, knowing he was a fool for doing this, but he walked back into the room and stood at the desk, across from his father. "Okay. Talk."

"How we're going to get your brother out of hot water? How we're going to turn this around so that the blame all falls on the other boy. It ought to be easy. We'll play up the fact that the other boy's a gypsy. That he's already been tried for swindling. We'll make it sound like Dominic swindled the money out of the company without Jeremy's involvement."

Preston couldn't believe what he was hearing. "What you're suggesting isn't going to work. It won't matter what I say. Every person on the team heard and saw what I did. I could go in there and lie my ass off, and it won't make one damned bit of difference. A U.S. Army colonel heard and saw the same shit I did. Who do you think they're going to believe? Me, the criminal's brother, or a colonel?"

His father sighed. "You don't have to go in and out and out lie. It's probably better if you don't. But you can tell the story so your brother doesn't sound so damn bad. I promise you the Kaslov woman will be doing the same for her brother. I'll have you both coached by then. He'll know what to say, and so will you. We're going to do everything we can to turn it around for him. He's your brother, and he damn near died over there. He doesn't need to sit in a fucking prison for years. He needs to take over the company. You need to do what you can to help him. Otherwise, there will be no one to run the company. Except you."

Preston knew this was the direction his father was going in, and the bad thing was his father had a point. If Jeremy was sitting in a prison cell, Ramos, Inc. would inevitably fall on Preston's shoulders. Right where he didn't want it. "I'll do what I can to save Jeremy's ass." Even if it left a sour taste in his mouth.

He was troubled as he left his father's office. He wouldn't lie, he told himself as he drove to the police station for his first shift since coming back. It would be stupid. Jeremy was going to prison no matter what the Ramos brothers said.

But maybe he could soften it some. Make it look more like it had all been Dominic's idea. When questioned, he could say that, unlike Dominic, Jeremy's record had been spotless until he fell under Dominic's spell.

He wondered what it said about him that he was going to help Jeremy try to paint a rosier picture of what had happened. All he knew was that right or wrong, his loyalty was to his family. He had nothing to lose.

Sabina had made it clear they were over.

Chapter Seventeen

Preston

Preston stopped at the base's entry and nodded at the young corporal standing guard. His ID sat on the passenger seat, and his police department badge was out too. He showed his license and badge to the corporal.

"I'm expected for a meeting with Colonel Bustamante," he said. "Army South building." He'd gotten an official letter overnighted to him on an NSA letterhead ordering him to report this morning, instructing him he was to say nothing to anyone about the mission in Colombia, and that any information he shared would be considered a breach of national security. His irate father had also gotten one instructing him not to talk to anyone and not to bring in his own lawyers as Jeremy would be provided legal services by attorneys with security clearance.

"They expect me to sit back and do nothing," his father had fumed. "Jeremy needs counsel."

"Dad, this isn't some open trial in a court of law," Preston had said impatiently. "Besides, you were warned before you insisted I go to Colombia there were government secrets that had to be kept. You made the deal," he added, holding up his hand when his father started to object. "You'll keep it, or you'll be sitting in a jail cell right next to Jeremy."

"But you both need coaching," his father had sputtered. "You know those government lawyers aren't going to look out for him."

"I don't know that, and neither do you."

Roel had descended on Jeremy's room at the hospital, prepared to spend hours coaching him, going over his story and looking for places they could make Dominic look bad, and was furious when Jeremy's nurse threw him out after thirty minutes.

"You can come back when he's better," the hard-nosed major informed him as she escorted him to the door. Roel had to content himself with the knowledge that Jeremy was prepared to incriminate Dominic and cry victim every chance he got. Preston wasn't surprised. Even though Jeremy loved Dominic enough to save him, neither of them could be trusted, and they both knew it.

Preston's father had sat him down for a similar coaching session, but Preston bowed out after fifteen minutes, telling his father he didn't have to be taught how to lie, and went home and finished a six-pack.

The corporal checked his name against a list and waved him through. The GPS guided Preston to a building he thought was the old hospital. A smartly uniformed receptionist directed him to the sixth floor. "You'll see everybody at the end of the hall."

He took the elevator to the sixth floor where a small crowd milled around at one end. There was no sign of his brother, not that he expected there to be. Jeremy was at the Army hospital with an armed guard at his door. He'd gone through four surgeries already, one on each broken leg, a third for internal injuries, and a fourth, which would be one of many on his badly damaged face. Whatever information they'd gotten from him had been from his hospital bed.

Preston could only imagine what his brother had told them.

It took him a moment to recognize Jazz and Eagle in their dress uniforms, sitting with two men in civilian suits and a couple of uniformed officers he didn't recognize.

They had their heads together, but no one seemed to be concerned about being overheard as he approached. Eagle spotted him and nodded. Jazz gave him a subtle nod as he sat across from them. A guard stood at a wide door, presumably leading to the meeting room.

Another knot of people milled around a little farther down. Preston spotted Dominic, who was wearing handcuffs and stood with a guard on either side of him, talking earnestly with another couple of men in civilian suits. His movements were stiff, his face pale and pinched.

Huh. Probably worried about what I'm going to say in the debriefing.

Once again it crossed his mind to wonder what Dominic and Sabina would say when questioned. He dismissed the thought, telling himself it was of no concern to him. They'd do as their conscience dictated, and he'd say what he could to paint a favorable picture of his brother.

Even if his conscience pricked him for it.

He sat impatiently as the minutes clicked by. Ten, fifteen, and then a half hour passed. Finally, the door opened, and a man in a general's uniform stepped out, followed by Colonel Bustamante, Colonel Johnson, and Paco, who was dressed in a sergeant's uniform.

A couple of lower-ranking officers followed them out, and after a pause, Sabina appeared. It was the first time he'd seen her in dress greens and her beret, and he had to admit she cut a striking figure.

She nodded solemnly and disappeared for a moment, returning with two power bars and a couple of sodas. "They're breaking for lunch, but it won't be long enough to go anywhere. Maybe this will help."

"Thanks." Preston took the power bar she offered and one of the sodas. She opened the other bar and nibbled a chunk off the top. He stared over at her, drinking in the sight. It'd been almost a week since he'd seen her, and that day she'd been disheveled and exhausted.

Today she was resplendent in her uniform, her hair pulled back in a neat bun and her face carefully made up. She looked rested, if not relaxed. Which was understandable if she'd put in a morning of debriefing. He glanced over at her brother, who was seated at the end of the hall, eating a sandwich. Again he wondered what she'd done: protected her brother or told the truth.

He couldn't tell anything from her expression.

They munched their bars and sipped their drinks in silence. She made no move to get up and join her brother. Not even a look passed between them.

It made him wonder if she'd talked to her family and refused to help him, and it had made them angry.

The brass returned thirty minutes later. Sabina followed them into the conference room and shut the door behind her. Preston sat for another hour, growing more impatient by the minute. He had a shift to work and had to leave by fourteen hundred.

He checked the time on his phone. At thirteen hundred forty-five, he approached the guard at the door. "I have to leave. I'm due at work in a little over an hour."

"Tell him." The guard pointed out one of the suits now talking to Eagle and Paco.

Preston approached the suit. "I have to be at work in less than an hour," he said. "Are they going to talk to me today, or aren't they?"

The suit looked unhappy. "You were told to report today, were you not?"

"I was also told to report to work." He gestured to Paco and Eagle. "This is these gentlemen's jobs. It's not mine."

The suit hoisted himself up off the bench and disappeared into the room. He appeared a moment later with Sabina trailing after him. "Change of plan. They'll see you tomorrow morning at ten. Plan to stay all day."

Preston nodded wearily. He started for the elevator, and Sabina fell into step beside him. He waited until they got in the elevator and were descending before he spoke.

"Taking a break?" he asked.

She shook her head. "They're through with me for the day. I have a class to teach at fifteen hundred."

"You have to go back tomorrow?"

"Probably for several days. The debriefs are thorough, especially for a mission as complicated as this one turned out to be. They gave Colonel Johnson a hard time."

"For saving Jeremy?"

"Yes. The general said she risked the team unnecessarily. Colonel Bustamante stuck up for her. Especially when we told them about Jeremey shining the flashlight in the senator's face."

"So does that mean they'll go easy on my brother?" he asked quietly.

"No, it means they forgave the colonel. I have no idea what they're going to say or do about Jeremy."

"What about Dominic?"

"What about him?"

"Surely you did what you could to protect him." He turned to her. "He's your brother. Surely you did something for him."

"I guess you could say I did." The elevator hit the ground floor, and they walked out of the building into the bright sunshine. "I told him to man up and tell the truth."

Preston stopped in his tracks. "What good is that going to do? He's as guilty as sin. If he admits to it, he'll sit in jail until he's an old man."

"If he lies under oath, he'll sit even longer. Preston, my brother broke the law in two countries and got involved with something affecting national security, all to make a quick buck. I've said all along I wasn't going to lie for him, and I'm not." She backed up and looked at him disbelievingly. "Don't tell me that's what you plan to do."

"The decision wasn't up to me. My father—"

"Your father, my ass. Let me spell it out for you. When you walk in there, you're going to be told to raise your right hand. You're going to swear to tell the truth. If you don't, if you go in there and lie your head off to protect your brother, you're gonna be charged with lying under oath. Don't you and your father realize that? If your story doesn't match ours perfectly, they'll know damned well you're the one lying." She shook her head. "Fuck a duck. I didn't think you were that stupid, even when Colonel Johnson had to pull the gun on you."

"I'm not going to go in there and lie. But if I can say something that shows Jeremy in a better light, I'm going to say it." He took a breath. "I never said I'd put my country before the welfare of my family. Damn few people would, and I'm not one of them."

The look she gave him was one of pure contempt. "Instead, you're going to sit there and implicate Dominic every chance you get, never mind that Dominic's going in and telling the truth. Let's blame the Romani. Hey, he's one of those lying, thieving gypsies. Let's pin it all on him, no matter what the truth happens to be. How'm I doin'?"

Preston flinched at the verbal attack. "I...I—"

"And Daddy's behind it, right? He says jump, and you ask how high. He says use your position with the police department to investigate Ramos business, you do it. He says drop everything and run to Colombia to protect your asshole of a brother, you do it. He tells you to fucking lie under oath and risk a prison sentence, you do it. What the fuck, Preston? You're thirty-eight years old. When are you going to grow up and quit jumping when Daddy says boo?"

"You have no right—"

"Shut. Up. I have every right." Her eyes blazed with passion and disgust. "Don't even try to defend your actions. They're not defensible." Her eyes flicked up and down. "You know, you're a piece of shit if there ever was one. You have the nerve to look down your nose on the Romani. You're trying to shelter a damned criminal in the family. Lying to protect him. Shading it so Jeremy doesn't look so bad. To hell with national security, loyalty to your country, the truth. To hell with the stockholders who bought into Ramos, Incorporated."

He took a step back, and she advanced on him. "And don't give me a load of crap about owing your family. You think my family's happy right now? Mom and Dad are furious with me, and Uncle

Milo says he'll never speak to me again. But you know what? I value my integrity. It's a shame you can't say the same." She took a breath. "You know what? It's not the Romani clan who's guilty of lying and being dishonorable. It's the Ramos family. It's *you*."

She turned away and walked off.

Preston stood shaken by her tirade, stunned by her brutality as word after word cut him to the core. His gut roiled, and for a moment he thought he'd be sick.

He stumbled to his truck and started the engine. His guilty conscience, simmering beneath the surface since he'd gone to Colombia, exploded.

Someone he cared deeply for had laid him open and exposed every single flaw he'd denied. Called him out on every moral failing, forcing him to take a hard, painful look at himself.

Why he couldn't do it himself made what she said more gut-wrenching.

He hated what he'd become.

Before he allowed his father to twist him up inside, in his heart, he'd known what he needed to do.

And he knew it now.

Chapter Eighteen

Sabina

Sabina wished the last of her students a good evening and dragged herself to her car. It was almost seventeen hundred, but the debriefings were most likely still going on. Some of the National Security Agency people conducting the debriefings had flown in from DC and didn't want to stay in San Antonio any longer than they had to. They'd made it known they were willing to work well into the evening. They were noticeably annoyed with Preston for not waiting, and she wouldn't be surprised if his questioning tomorrow was brutal.

Which was perfectly all right with her. They could be as brutal as they wanted with the SOB. She'd like to do more to him than subjecting him to a bruising question-and-answer session. She would love to string him up by those balls of his and let him swing in the breeze.

Her eyes started to water, and she brushed away the tears with trembling fingers.

I should've known better than to have any faith in him.

She headed across the base toward the Army South lot where her car was parked, wishing she'd driven to her classroom rather than stomping across the base in fury after she'd ripped him a new one.

What if he managed to make his brother look good at the expense of hers? She was terrified her insistence on telling the truth, and Preston's determination not to, would cost her brother an even higher price than he was already going to have to pay.

She started to get in her car, but the lot was still full, and she recognized the vehicles belonging to the rest of her team.

Perhaps I should find out a bit more about how tomorrow might go.

She made a beeline for the building and took the elevator to the sixth floor. Paco and Eagle were nowhere to be seen, neither were Dominic or the colonels, but some of the NSA officials were sitting together at the end of the hall, conferring. They looked up, recognized her, nodded and smiled before going back to their confab.

She sat down far enough away so she wouldn't be guilty of eavesdropping. Her discussion with Preston had seriously upset her. She wanted reassurance from somebody that she and Dominic were doing the right thing. Maybe one of the colonels would be willing to talk to her, have some words of wisdom. Even if they didn't, it wouldn't hurt them to know what Preston was planning to do.

Almost an hour passed before the door opened, and General McKinley strode out, followed by Paco and Eagle. If they were surprised to see her, it didn't show. Instead, they smiled tiredly as they headed for the elevator, and she'd bet a week's pay they ended up in Paco's apartment with beers and pizza.

If she hadn't wanted to talk to one of the colonels so much, she would've joined them.

Instead, she waited another fifteen minutes until Colonel Johnson and Colonel Bustamante walked out. She rose with a salute for any onlookers. They acknowledged her with nods and smiles. "You're still here," Colonel Johnson said. "I thought you had a class to teach."

"I came back." Sabina swallowed. "Do either of you have a minute? I need to talk to someone."

Apparently, her expression was troubled enough that the colonels looked at one another and nodded. "I believe we can spare you a few minutes," Colonel Bustamante said. "Come down to my office."

They walked down the hall to his sixth-floor office. His administrative aide was already gone, so he shut the outer door and ushered them into his private office. Colonel Johnson got them bottled water from a small fridge, and they turned to Sabina. "What's on your mind?" Colonel Johnson asked.

Sabina took a deep breath. "Not sure where to begin." She looked across the desk at Colonel Bustamante and then over to Colonel Johnson. "How much…what if… Preston's planning to go in there and paint my brother in the worst possible light to try to make it look better for Jeremy? How seriously can what he says influence what happens to Dominic?"

"Not at all," Colonel Bustamante said.

"None whatsoever," Colonel Johnson added. She pursed her lips. "Why? Is the idiot planning to go in there and lie? Because he'll be in deep shit if he does."

"Not lie, he's not that stupid."

"Couldn't tell it by me," Colonel Johnson said, her lips twitching.

"I'd have paid good money to see her pull her gun on him," Colonel Bustamante added, deadpan.

"Let's say that from then on, when I spoke, he listened." Colonel Johnson snickered, but then her face sobered. "Go on, Sabina."

"I thought he was coming around, after what he'd seen and heard Jeremy do. That he understood how serious Jeremy's crimes were and how deeply involved his brother was in the smuggling. But then he got home, and his father got hold of him again and persuaded him he needed to finesse his story, make it sound like Dominic took advantage of Jeremy, pin it on the Romani boy." Sabina's lips twisted. "I told Dominic to tell the truth. And now Preston's planning to go in there and make him look even worse. Did I make a mistake? I can't help but think I hurt my brother by telling him to be honest."

Colonel Johnson shook her head. "You didn't hurt your brother in the least. Those NSA guys weren't born yesterday; they're not stupid, and they can smell a lie from a mile away. So can General McKinley and the rest of the Army brass.

"Believe me, it's to your brother's advantage for the both of you to be completely forthcoming. As far as the Ramos brothers go, I've read Jeremy's deposition, and I swear the boy has a future in fiction writing. Every word of which was contradicted by either your testimony, mine, or one of the other team members. If Preston goes in there telling the same kind of half-truths, they'll see through him too. Besides, this isn't a trial. It's a mission debriefing. Quite a different thing."

"Come on, Sabina, you know all this," Colonel Bustamante chided. "Besides, why do you care what that cop says or does? He's the last person on the planet who you should give a thought to."

"I know," Sabina murmured, even as her face heated up. "I just thought—" She flushed.

The two colonels exchanged a look. "Oh." Colonel Bustamante's eyebrow shot almost to his hairline.

Colonel Johnson patted Sabina's arm. "You fell for him, and he disappointed you."

"I did, and yes." Sabina raised her head. "I thought… Never mind what I thought. He's the man I first judged him to be, not the man I thought I knew in Colombia. A colossal error in judgment on my part."

"Well, now you know," Colonel Bustamante said softly. "So, back to your brother. Don't give it another thought. You and Dominic are the ones doing the right thing. Not the Ramos brothers. If you like, I can arrange for you to be present when they debrief Dominic. It might be good for both of you if you were there for moral support."

"Thank you, Colonel. I'd like that. And thank you too, Colonel Johnson. I'll sleep better tonight." The colonels wished her a good evening and signaled she could go.

She was deep in thought as she walked to her car. Conflicting emotions swirled in her head. Relief, certainly. If the colonels were correct, she and Dominic's unvarnished honesty would be to her brother's advantage. It was the crushing disappointment that hurt the most.

She'd fallen for a man who didn't exist. The Preston Ramos she'd come to have feelings for in Colombia had been a lie. Her first impressions of him had been correct.

She picked up a pizza and ice cream on the way home and demolished all of it. Her sleep was troubled, partly by indigestion and partly by an unfortunate tendency to dream about her and Preston tangled up together in bed.

***

The next morning, it took a hot shower and three cups of coffee before she could clear her head enough to face the day.

As she got off the elevator on the sixth floor, the brass was assembling. Dominic was back, sitting with his two guards on a bench at the end of the hall. She walked over and leaned down and squeezed his hand. "You go in this morning, right?"

Dominic nodded. "I'm going in there and digging my own grave."

Sabina bit her lip. It would do no good at this late date to point out it was his own damned fault. "You're going in there to tell the truth so you don't make it worse for yourself," she said briskly. "Colonel Bustamante said I could go in there with you for moral support, if you'd like me to."

Her brother nodded. "Yeah, I'd like that."

General McKinley and the NSA officers strode down the hall at precisely zero seven fifty-five. Colonel Bustamante and Colonel Johnson were behind them, followed by more of the Army brass.

Dominic's suits motioned to the guards, and they escorted him into the conference room and seated him about halfway down the long conference table. The Army brass and NSA officers filled up the rest of the seats. Sabina was motioned to a chair against the wall since she was there for moral support rather than to testify. The recorders were turned on, and the lead NSA questioner turned to Dominic.

"State your name, address, and date of birth for the record, please." Dominic did so. "Raise your right hand. Do you swear to tell the truth this morning?" Dominic's affirmative answer rang through the room. "Now, Mr. Kaslov, tell us what led up to your decision to go to Colombia and steal tens of thousands of dollars of raw emeralds."

And so it began. One answer at a time, Dominic took them through the entire sorry episode, from seeing a YouTube video made by a successful *guaquero* touting his success, to their encounter with the senator and how it all went sideways.

Sabina listened to every word her brother said, every tone and inflection, paying special attention when he discussed Jeremy's role in the scam. He was forthcoming about where and how they met, their common interest in making a fast buck, and Jeremy's role in the whole plan. He whitewashed nothing.

Despite what he'd done and the trouble he'd caused, Sabina couldn't help but be proud of her little brother.

At nearly twelve hundred one of the Army officers asked Dominic his last question. Then he was taken from the room while everyone else at the table finished up with their notes.

"Well, that was refreshing," General McKinley said. "He didn't try to lie or cover up a single thing." He nodded to Sabina, approval written all over his face.

She nodded back.

The Army brass and NSA officers rose and filed out, followed by Colonel Bustamante and Colonel Johnson. Sabina was one of the last out, only to practically stumble over Preston, who was standing in the middle of the hall with his phone glued to his ear.

"No, Dad, they haven't called me in yet. Yes, Dad. I can stay today. I switched shifts with one of the guys on the eleven to seven." He was quiet for a minute. "Yes, yes, I know what to say and do.

Talk to you later." He clicked off the phone and put it in his pocket. Only then did he spot Sabina as her gaze bored into him.

So the bastard is going to do it. Preston was going to go in there and say whatever he thought would paint his brother in a more favorable light. Sabina started to say something to him, but the general's words had her closing her mouth.

Just leave it. He won't change his mind.

She held her head up high and marched past Preston as she headed to the elevators, dismissing him with a glance of contempt she hoped spoke volumes.

Let him go in there and try to finesse the truth. Let him repeat every damned lie Roel Ramos coached him to say. It was his own grave he was digging. His and Jeremy's.

She hoped he dug a nice deep one.

Chapter Nineteen
Preston

If looks could kill, he'd be a goner.

Preston rubbed his hand across his eyes and watched Sabina march down the hall and jab the elevator button. She was mad as a hornet, which didn't surprise him. His buzzing brain had replayed her angry but truthful tirade over and over for most of the night. But today he could see disappointment in her eyes. He hadn't lived up to her standards. He hadn't been the man she thought he was.

If she was going to do the right thing, she had every reason to expect him to do the same.

Preston sighed and sat down on the bench. One of the suits had explained he would be debriefed as soon as everyone got back from lunch and said he was free to find a meal. But no way was he hungry.

He'd eaten a late breakfast, which sat heavily on his stomach, and he was within an inch of puking it up. He'd go throw up deliberately if he thought it would do something to quell the queasiness.

The upcoming debriefing was more than a simple afternoon of testimony. He was at a crossroads in his life. The next couple of hours were crucial, and no matter what he did, there was going to be a high price to pay.

The general and the brass returned and filed into the room. A couple of minutes later, one of the suits stuck his head out the door. "We're ready for you, Mr. Ramos."

Preston nodded and followed the man into the conference room. Colonel Bustamante gestured to a chair about halfway down the table. One of the suits asked Preston his name, address, and birthdate for the record. He was asked to stand and raise his right hand. "Do you swear to tell the truth this afternoon?"

The words echoed in Preston's brain. He was vowing to tell the plain, unvarnished truth. Not the pack of half-lies his father had tried to shove down his throat less than an hour ago.

He was going to tell the truth, even knowing his father and the consequences Preston would face.

"I do."

He sat at the table. His hands trembled, and he stuffed them into his lap as he looked around at the faces staring back at him. Faces, for the most part, he didn't know except for Colonel Bustamante and Colonel Johnson, who regarded him with apparent disappointment and resignation.

Well, hell. Sabina must've told them what he'd said to her earlier. He didn't blame them one bit. He held up his head, and one at a time, looked every person at the table in the eye. "I'm ready."

One of the civilians looked down at his iPad. "We'll start at the beginning. When did you first learn your brother was in Colombia in the company of Dominic Kaslov?"

Preston told them everything, as honestly as he knew how. Every facet of the event, from the first message from Jeremy to say he was out of the country, to his brother's part in the affair and his unexpected heroism in pushing Dominic out of the way and being captured. Preston gave them everything.

He thanked Colonel Johnson for saving Jeremy. "I know it's not what you would've recommended," he said to General McKinley. "But he's my brother, and I love him. And despite everything he did, and all the laws he broke, he did enable Captain Begay to get a clearer picture of the senator in the dark."

Finally, he admitted Jeremy had been behind the scam bilking Ramos, Inc. out of the ten million. Preston knew he had an apology to make to Sabina, and it needed to be made soon.

The lead questioner looked down at his notes. "Mr. Ramos, do you have any idea why your brother would engage in these kinds of illegal activities? He didn't need to defraud the company or steal emeralds. He comes from a wealthy family, and everyone has said your brother was your father's heir apparent. Did he ever indicate what his motivation was?"

Preston felt his face flush with shame. "He said it was because he could."

The questioner nodded solemnly and looked around the table. Most of the other suits looked at him impassively. The only ones who had any expression at all were the two colonels and General McKinley, who all looked surprised.

They'd expected him to lie, but he'd proved he had a spine and he could make his own decisions.

General McKinley cleared his throat. "If no one has any other questions, we want to thank you this afternoon for coming in for this debriefing. We appreciate your candor."

His face flaming, Preston wished them all a good day and left the room. He collapsed on one of the benches and pulled his silenced phone out of his pocket. His father had put in three calls to him during the debriefing. He looked at the phone and wondered what the hell to say.

He was tempted to lie and say he'd done what his father asked. But this was only the first of many times he'd have to tell this story. There would be more debriefings, and at some point, he'd be questioned in a court of law. His father was eventually going to find out Preston had been truthful and hadn't covered his little brother's ass. He was going to be in deep shit with Roel sooner or later.

It might as well be today.

He took a deep breath and punched in his father's private line. "How did it go?" his father demanded.

"It went."

"You know what I mean. Did they appear to buy your story? Were you able to get Jeremy out of trouble?"

"No, I didn't. He's still in a lot of trouble."

"Why? Didn't your testimony help?"

"I doubt it. I told the truth."

"You *what?*"

Preston flinched and held his phone away from his ear. His father's screech of fury had everyone in the hall staring at him. He glanced around in embarrassment before putting the phone back to his ear. "I told the truth. I didn't sugarcoat or try to whitewash anything. I told it like it was."

"You told it like it was." His father's voice dripped with contempt. "Do you mean that after I told you exactly what you needed to do, you went in there and did something else? *What the hell were you thinking?*"

Preston took a deep breath. "I was thinking I needed to do the right thing, that lying to my government to save my criminal brother wasn't especially moral or smart. I was thinking that by lying, I was acting like the Romani you despise so much, and I didn't want to do that." He paused a minute. "I was thinking the Romani you hate so much are the ones doing the right thing. Not us."

"You...you...damn it to hell, Preston. Your brother could sit in jail for years, thanks to you and your bullshit. If he does, it will be your fault. You asshole. You *pendejo.*"

"So it's all my fault," Preston said mildly. "Never mind he stole tens of thousands of dollars of emeralds and broke the laws of two countries. Never mind he stole ten million from your company. It's all my fault because I wouldn't lie for the little bastard."

"Yes, it's your fault," his father snapped. "Damn it, I don't care what Jeremy's done. I need him to take over the damned company for us, for the family, and for the company you turned your back on. I sent you down there to protect this family's interests, and you didn't."

"You mean you sent me down there to get my ass killed taking care of your precious criminal baby." Preston's voice started to harden. "You didn't give a damn about how much danger you put me in, so long as *Jeremy* was protected. You've expected me to jump through your fucking hoops for years. All for Ramos, Inc. You've used me for the last time. I told the truth about Jeremy, and I plan to keep right on doing it."

His father gasped. He was silent for so long, Preston wondered if he'd hung up. Finally, his father spoke. "This was the last goddamned straw. You've let me down for the last fucking time. You're dead to me and to this entire family. *You're no son of mine.*" He clicked off before Preston had a chance to answer.

With trembling fingers, he shoved his phone in his pocket. "Well, there went Christmas dinner," he muttered through the lump in his throat.

"Nah. He'll change his mind."

Preston looked up, startled, to see the two colonels standing before him. "You heard."

"Everybody in the hall heard," Colonel Johnson said. "You know he didn't mean it."

"That's just it. He did." Preston ran his hand down the side of his face. "You don't know my father. I've pissed him off once too often. As far as he's concerned, I'm now dead."

"Your mother?" Colonel Bustamante asked.

"She won't buck him." Preston stood up. "That's why it was so hard to go in there and do what I did. I've lost my whole family as a result," he choked out.

The colonels were silent for a minute. "I'm so sorry," Colonel Johnson said gently. "At least you have Sabina."

Preston laughed harshly. "No, I don't. She's so disillusioned with me, I doubt she'll ever give me the time of day again."

"Would it be any consolation if I pointed out that you did the right thing?" Colonel Bustamante said.

"It's the only consolation I have. Doing the right thing takes a weight off my shoulders. But it's also going to be damned lonely."

"Sometimes doing the right thing is lonely," Colonel Bustamante agreed.

"But maybe it doesn't have to be." Colonel Johnson looked thoughtful.

He wondered what the hell she meant by that.

They wished him a good afternoon, and he wandered out to his car. Well, it was two for two, he thought morosely as he started the engine. He'd managed to permanently alienate Sabina yesterday and his family today. He was going to miss his family, no doubt. His father was a jerk, but he was still his father. And his spineless mother was caught in the middle.

But they weren't the ones putting the cramp in his stomach. It was Sabina. He'd fallen for her, and even if their relationship was over, he still cared about what she thought of him.

Right now, she probably thought he was lower than whale shit. Which stung. A lot.

He'd apologize to her, for all the good it would do.

A drink would be good about now. Hell, a whole bottle would, but he had to report for the graveyard shift, and he couldn't show up to work drunk.

His job was all he had left at this point, and he'd be damned if he did anything to risk it.

He didn't have to clock in downtown until twenty-two hundred, and there were a lot of empty hours between now and then, so he swung by the building supply store and bought enough paint to put at least one coat on the back bedroom.

He didn't know if painting would be enough to calm his nerves or lower his blood pressure—or get Sabina off his mind—but if nothing else, his back bedroom would look a lot better when he was done.

Chapter Twenty
Sabina

Sabina wished the last of her students a good evening as they walked out the door. It had been a long and painful day, even more so than yesterday, and she was ready for another round of bad nutrition and schlocky television. Maybe a bit of retail therapy would help. The Dillard's at the mall was running a gift with purchase in her favorite makeup line, and maybe it was time to treat herself. Or she could bite the bullet and go swimsuit shopping. Crawling in and out of swimsuits, trying to choose the most flattering, would take her mind off just about anything. She didn't know if it would work with Dominic and Preston in her head twenty-four seven, but it was worth a try.

Her phone buzzed, and she looked at the screen and made a face. She'd ignored calls from her family for several days now, not wanting to get into anymore arguments with them. The last exchange with her father, the night before she was due to debrief, was contentious in the extreme.

"Damn it, you need to help your brother," her father had demanded. "I don't care what he's done. He's your brother, and you need to help him."

She tried arguing, but nothing she said made any difference. She told them she'd talk to them when they were ready to be reasonable and had hung up in frustration. She hadn't talked to them since.

I suppose it's time to tell them what happened. They'll either understand or they won't.

She swiped to answer.

"Took you long enough," her father snapped. "We were about to get in the car and come to San Antonio. Did you come to your senses about Dominic?"

Sabina rolled her eyes. "Are you ready to listen to me now? Or should I hang up again?"

"No. Wait. At least tell me what's going on."

"Dominic and I have been debriefed. We went in and told the truth as best we could. The brass appreciated our candor."

"How do you know?" her father asked suspiciously.

"Because the general came out and said so."

Her father took a minute to process that. "What about Dominic?"

"He broke the laws in two countries. He helped his buddy swindle ten million dollars from a San Antonio company. He'll have to answer for it."

Her father let loose with a string of swear words. "And you wouldn't do a damn thing to help him."

"What would you have me do, Dad? Lie under oath? Have him lie under oath?" Sabina took a deep breath. "I have a question for you. All my life you and Mom stressed that the Kaslov family were decent, law-abiding Americans. That we weren't like the stereotypes. That people who viewed us negatively were wrong. Were you lying to me? Was it all horse shit? Are we going to be like people think of us after all? Was that cop justified in his prejudice?"

"But it's your brother," her father protested. "You could've made an exception for him."

"So, do we really mean it about living differently, or are there forever going to be exceptions?"

Her father sucked in his breath. He was quiet, and she could sense the wheels turning in his head. "You're right. We can't make exceptions. Even when it's one of our own. It's just...damn it, that's my son who's going to jail. It hurts. It hurts so damn bad." She could hear her father break down and start to cry.

Tears welled. "I know, Daddy. It just about killed me to go in there and tell them what he'd done."

She could hear him crying on the other end of the line. "I know, baby girl. I know it did."

She sat knotted up inside and listened to him sob.

Finally, she could hear him trying to get himself together. It took some time, but his crying finally subsided. "How is he?"

"Exhausted. Resigned to his fate. He also knows his lover tried to lie his way out of trouble by putting all the blame on him."

"Lover?"

Oh, shit. She hadn't told her parents about that.

"Jeremy."

"Jeremy was his lover? The other man? You mean the one who saved him? Well, hell."

"Right now, Dominic's love life is the least of anybody's worries."

"Whatever." Her father cleared his throat. "Tell your brother we'll come see him soon. Can he have visitors in jail?"

"I imagine. I'll find out for sure."

He was quiet for a minute. "How are *you* doing, honey?"

She'd been better, but she wasn't going to tell him that. She assured him she was doing okay, hanging in fine, and encouraged him to bring her mother to San Antonio to see her and Dominic. He wished her a good evening, and they disconnected.

She wiped the remaining tears from her eyes. Her father had come around, exactly as she'd hoped he would. His initial reaction was to protect Dominic, but he'd given way to his rock-solid integrity. There was a reason for her bone-deep belief in right and wrong and sense of morality, and despite what she'd told Preston, her Army oath had little to do with it. She'd learned it at home from her mother and father.

It was a shame Preston hadn't learned the same lesson.

She was glad she and her father had come to an understanding. But she still could use a dose of retail therapy.

She ran up the stairs to her office, prepared to grab her purse and hit the parking lot. The young corporal serving as administrative aide to the instructors nodded toward her office. "You have a visitor. A significant one," he said knowingly. "Waiting in your office."

That was weird. The only significant visitors she might've had were her team members, and while she knew damned well Corporal Farley suspected she was more than a simple instructor, they'd never spoken of it.

She thanked him and headed into her office, only to nearly stop in her tracks to find Colonel Johnson waiting for her. Her mind raced. While the detachment commanders were more accessible to them than most officers in a chain of command, it was almost unheard of for them to meet with their team members in their offices. They always met in the brass's office. But Colonel Johnson's smile put her at ease as she saluted her commander.

"Have a seat, Sabina." Colonel Johnson gestured to Sabina's desk chair.

"Yes, Colonel." Sabina sat down uncertainly. She didn't know what to think. Presumably Colonel Johnson had something she wanted to say or she wouldn't be here, so Sabina waited for her commander to speak.

"I'm not here this afternoon as your commander, Sabina. I'm here as your friend, and I hope, your mentor."

"Yes, ma'am." Now Sabina was truly baffled. This was highly unusual, even for the members of Bear's Brigade.

The colonel smiled faintly. "Mr. Ramos testified this afternoon. He told the truth after all. Complete and unvarnished. And the poor bastard paid a high price for it."

Sabina sat up straight. "He did? He told the truth?"

"He did. He didn't try to whitewash or finesse a single thing. His testimony matched everyone else's."

"Except for Jeremy's."

"Yes, except for Jeremy's elaborate work of fiction."

Sabina's head spun. "That's not what he told me he was going to do."

"No, it isn't. Honestly, I was surprised, and so was Bear. I think the general was too."

"I'm glad. I didn't know he had it in him. I thought he was so far under his father's influence he would do whatever his father told him to, regardless."

"He didn't. He told the truth. The general thanked him for his candor."

"I'm glad the general was appreciative."

Colonel Johnson made a face. "Not everyone was as grateful. His father disowned him. Told him outright he was dead to him. Preston said that was why it was so hard for him to do the right thing. Because he knew what his father would do."

"I imagine his father will come around. Mine did."

"I don't think his father will. Roel Ramos must be a real piece of work."

"He is."

"Preston also said you'd written him off."

Sabina felt her face flush. "I did, and I let him know it. I was hard on him yesterday when he told me what he planned to do."

"And now?"

She looked down at her hands. "Our relationship was over anyway. It was a moment out of time. A moment that's over."

"Even though you fell head over heels for each other." Sabina's head popped up, and she looked at the colonel with surprise. "Don't try to deny it, Sabina. I have eyes." Colonel Johnson looked faintly amused. "You fell for Preston, and he fell for you just as hard. Why do you think I kept my mouth shut when you chose to stay with him at the safe house? I wasn't about to get in the way of something so real."

"It was real. But back in the world, we have a lot of strikes against us."

"Strikes against you. Hmm. I don't think you know what really constitutes strikes against you." Colonel Johnson's face took on a faraway look. "Try falling for a white corporal when you're not only a Black woman in the Army, but a first lieutenant and still haven't proven yourself. Throw in a couple of bigoted majors and a family whose Black pride is a wall as much as a source of solidarity. Then get pregnant by the corporal. That's some strikes against you. But Jack and I would've made it, I firmly believe that." She trailed off, and her face sobered.

"Would've made it?" Sabina prompted.

"He died in combat before he could put a ring on my finger. I just about went down when I lost Jack, and if it hadn't been for Lemar, my son, I might have. My point is, if you and that man love each other the way I think you do, it wasn't a moment out of time. It's a helluva lot more. And remember this: despite some of the things he's done that weren't so wonderful, he defied his father and did the right thing because you challenged him to, knowing it was going to cause a permanent breach within his family.

"I'm not saying he did it for you, or that you owe him for doing it. What I'm saying is that he's turning out to be the man you fell in love with in Colombia after all. A man you might be proud to have at your side."

"But what about the prejudice? He doesn't like Romani. I'm Romani, and so is my family."

"Doesn't like them or thought he didn't like them based on what he'd been taught as a child? When we first met, Jack had a bit of an attitude problem. One he'd picked up from his father. Once he got to know me and a few other Black people, his opinions changed. Besides, if Preston's rejecting the rest of his family's horse shit, he might be jettisoning their prejudice along with it. It wouldn't hurt to find out."

"How?"

"Go talk to him. He's convinced you'll never forgive him, so he's not going to reach out to you. You'll have to make the first move."

"So I should go to him and ask him point blank if he still hates and despises the Romani. Or my family."

"It's the only way you're ever going to know for sure. I'll admit it's a risk. But think about the days and nights you spent with him in Colombia and ask yourself if it might be a risk worth taking." Colonel Johnson checked her buzzing phone, and her face lit up. "Gotta go. Lemar and his boyfriend, Brody, just hit town and are making noises about cooking steak."

"At least you don't have far to go." Colonel Johnson lived in one of the historic old homes in the residential section across the base.

The colonel nodded. "I'll leave you now. Please think about it, Sabina. Love doesn't come along every day, and you'd be wise to embrace it when it does."

Sabina nodded. The colonel left while Sabina's brain was working overtime.

With no reason to stay, she gathered up her handbag and fled the base for the mall and the retail therapy she'd promised herself. She hit Dillard's for the gift with purchase and looked at swimsuits in a couple of stores but didn't see anything she liked well enough to bother with trying on. She wasn't in the mood anyway.

She ordered up a plate of mediocre moo goo gai pan in the food court and ate it while indulging in a bit of people watching.

Every good-looking, dark-haired man reminded her of Preston and of the nights she'd spent in his arms. Of the way she felt when he made love to her. Of the man who loved his brother enough to go on a risk-filled mission to keep him safe, and the man who wanted to protect his brother as much as she wanted to protect hers.

The man who'd told the truth today and done what was right, permanently alienating his entire family.

She'd thought she'd never forgive him for what he'd almost done.

Sabina finished her egg roll and tossed the rest of the moo goo gai pan in the trash. The colonel was right. Sabina had fallen in love with Preston. Not the racist asshole of their initial encounters, but the good, decent man she'd gotten to know in Colombia during their moment out of time. If the colonel was right, he'd fallen for her too.

She owed it to herself to go talk to him.

If he was the man she hoped he was, she'd be foolish to pass up the chance of happiness.

She'd spent longer in the mall than she'd planned, and the sun was slipping below the horizon when she pulled onto Preston's street. His truck was in the narrow driveway, so she parked along the curb. Doubt flooded her mind. What if this was the wrong decision?

Her heart pounded, and she almost started the engine to drive away. But if she did, she'd never know if her fears were justified. Instead, she marched up to the front door and took a deep breath as she rang the bell.

He didn't come to the door for the longest time, and she wondered if he'd seen her car and decided not to answer. She was about to give up and leave when he pulled open the front door. The last two days had taken a toll on him. His face was drawn, and his eyes were shadowed. He was beaten down and it showed.

Yet, he'd never looked more precious.

His ratty T-shirt and jeans were spattered with paint, and he held a paint-covered rag in his hands. Hope flared in his eyes for a moment but was quickly replaced by confusion.

"Sabina? What are you doing here?"

"Can I come in?"

"Sure." He held open the screen door, and she walked in, careful not to brush up against his clothes. But she could feel the warmth of his body and smell a bit of his aftershave beneath the paint and turpentine fumes.

He shut the door behind him. "Let me get out of these clothes."

"I didn't mean to disturb you. I can come back tomorrow."

"'S all right. I was packing up the painting stuff anyway. I need to get a shower and a sandwich before I go to work. Have a seat. I'll be right back."

He disappeared before she could answer. She walked into the living room and looked around, appreciating the clean lines of the old Deco home. It was almost sparsely furnished with good-quality leather and wood in a simple retro style complimenting the house.

No knickknacks distracted the eye, and the only artwork on the wall was a metal sculpture over the sofa. A flatscreen television graced the wall across from the oversized recliner on the far side of the sofa.

A laptop sat at one end of a heavy dining table off the main living room. A peek into the kitchen revealed countertops bare but for a coffee machine and a couple of pans on the stove. The entire front of the house screamed bachelor pad and reminded her of her own minimally furnished apartment.

Having satisfied her curiosity, she sat down on the comfortable sofa.

Preston reappeared a few minutes later, freshly showered and wearing his uniform pants and a tight tee. He carried his bullet-proof vest, not unlike the one they'd worn in Colombia. He plopped down beside her on the sofa, his expression as uncertain as hers.

"I'm glad to see you," he said quietly. "I don't know why you came, but I'm so glad you did." He looked at her with a soft expression. "I know we already said it was over. But then I started to hope maybe it wasn't, that there might be more for you and me. And then there was yesterday. I thought you'd never speak to me again."

"I thought I wouldn't either. I was pretty angry."

"With good reason. Are you still?"

"No. Colonel Johnson told me what you did. And what happened afterwards."

"Oh. That." He ran his hand down the side of his face. "My fucked-up family's not your problem. I knew what was going to happen if I was honest, and I did it anyway." He turned to her. "It's why I had such a hard time deciding to tell the truth instead of my father's whitewashed version of events. He's been pissed and disappointed in me for years, and today was the last straw. He officially threw me out of the family."

"Geez, what an ass-wipe. I'm sorry, Preston. I really am."

"They're jerks."

"Yeah, but they were your jerks, and you love them."

He let out a bark of laughter. "I suppose I do."

They were both silent for a minute. "I guess I should thank you," she said. "For not lying about Dominic. But that's not why I came."

"Then why did you come?"

"Because Colonel Johnson said to." She reached for his hand. "She could tell I love you, and she said you'd fallen for me too, and that what we had was more than a moment out of time and we needed to do something about it."

"She *what?*"

"She said we love each other and that love doesn't come along every day, and that we shouldn't pass it up."

"This is the same woman who would've put a bullet between my eyes?" he asked. She nodded. "I would've never dreamed the tough-as-nails colonel is a romantic at heart."

"She said it's why she didn't say anything about us sleeping together. I told her we had issues, and she said we needed to talk about them."

"Yeah, we do. But first, let me kiss you, Sabina. I've missed kissing you." He grasped her gently by the shoulders and pulled her up against him.

His lips were tender as he closed them over hers, gentle yet demanding as she could feel him pouring all he felt for her into the embrace. She slid her arms around his neck, welcoming his closeness as his mouth explored hers.

She opened her lips to grant him entrance, her fingers fisting in his hair as they shared the sweetest of kisses. This was more than a physical connection. Preston was kissing her with his heart and soul.

He was telling her in no uncertain terms what he felt for her, feelings he might not even be able to put into words. The same feelings she had for him.

They kissed and touched for long moments. She broke off the kiss and moved away from him.

"We still need to talk."

He ran his hand down the side of her face. "Yeah, we do." He turned away and stared into space. "Our brothers did some despicable things. I'll have to testify against your brother, and you'll have to testify against mine. And our testimony is a good part of what will put them in jail."

"That right there would be a dealbreaker for most couples," she said quietly.

"It would."

"And we have the other to deal with along with it," she murmured. "I'm Romani, and you don't like the Romani. After your dealings with Dominic, maybe for good reason." She shifted on the sofa. "Your family may have tossed you out, but I'm still part of mine and always will be. If it goes anywhere with us, they'll be part of your life too. How is that going to be for you?"

He was quiet and looked thoughtful. "I'm not so sure that's true. Me not liking Romani, I mean. In fact, I'm pretty sure it isn't. At least not anymore. You've opened my eyes to my prejudice."

Sabina smiled. "I'm glad I could change your mind."

"Mom and Dad were wrong," Preston admitted. "*I* was wrong. Most Romani are law-abiding citizens like you, people I can like and admire. If only I could be the same."

"The colonel said you already are. You went in there and told the truth, knowing you were going to pay a helluva price. A price I didn't have to pay. Dad said he knew I'd done the right thing. It broke his heart that I had to. Uncle Milo's still pissed off, but he'll come around sooner or later." She paused a minute. "So you're okay with Romani?"

"More than okay. The question is whether the Romani, particularly the Kaslov family, are okay with me. How much of the debacle does your family know about?"

"Enough. But they also understand how pervasive prejudice can be. You're not the first person they've had to forgive, and you won't be the last."

"But I also testified against their son and will have to again."

"So did I. You also testified against your own brother and didn't try to blame it all on Dominic. They'll be okay with you, Preston."

"Good. I wouldn't want them upset with me if we end up married."

"Married?" Sabina didn't try to hide her surprise. "We haven't even gone out on our first date."

"Which we'll remedy in short order. If you feel the same way about me that I feel about you, we most certainly could end up married. What we have is special, and I'm interested in taking it as far as it will go. Marriage, kids, the whole nine yards. Someday. In the meantime, we go out on dates and get to know each other and make sweet love every chance we get.

"You chase down bad guys with your hush-hush soldiers, and I do it on the streets of San Antonio. We treasure every moment we have together as we grow what we've started into something special. What do you say?"

"It's not going to be easy, at least not at first," she said slowly. "The situation with our brothers is going to be hanging over our heads for quite a while. But, yeah. I'm in. I love you. I want to grow what we have."

"I love you too." Preston smiled, and his eyes shone with unshed tears. "I wish I could make love to you all night, but duty calls. Another kiss before I go?"

She melted into his arms. Their kiss was a declaration and an affirmation.

And a sweet, sweet promise.

They'd already overcome so much.

They would continue to.

And they would do it together.

It was everything Sabina could hope for and more.

TAKE A SNEAK PEEK AT THE NEXT

BEAR'S BRIGADE STORY

Jazz turned the corner onto the street where Carrie Burke lived. Sure enough, she was packing her rattletrap old car with a worn duffle.

He pulled up in the driveway and parked behind her car as she came out of the house carrying another duffle and a food hamper. She glanced at him and popped open the trunk, and threw the duffle and hamper inside before turning to him.

"Why are you here?"

"I just happened to drop by?"

"Horse shit. You didn't happen to drop by. Just like you didn't happen to take me on a date last night. No, you're here about Joe. You pumped me all evening for information about him. It didn't snap until Felicia came over trying to throw her weight around. News flash: I finally smelled the rat. It didn't work for her, and it's not working for you. You need to move your car. I have to leave."

"No. You aren't going looking for your stepdad alone. You're coming with me."

"No."

"Damn it, Carrie. It's admirable of you to want to go down to Mexico and face who knows what to see to his welfare. But it's foolish in the extreme. You don't speak the language, and a *gringo* down there is exposed to all kinds of risk."

More risk than she realizes, he thought.

She had no idea her stepfather was an operative and that he'd most likely run afoul of the cartel. The woman was waltzing into a situation that could easily get her killed.

He was glad the government gave a damn about Joe and wanted to check on him, but he still wasn't happy about the colonel's orders for him to accompany Carrie on the trip.

She had no business going down there.

Not that he or anyone else could tell her why.

Her family had tried to discourage her from going. Felicia, the colonel's sweetie, had tried to talk her out of it and been told to stuff it. Carrie was tired of everyone thinking of her as a pushover and had told Felicia as much with a lot of colorful language.

Given the Army couldn't detain her, they'd ordered him to go with her.

Anger flared in her eyes. "Tough shit. I'm going. Alone.

"Look, Jazz, I have no doubt my brother Harlan and his female posse sent you over here thinking you're going to fucking push me around. Ain't gonna work. I've had it with them, and with you, and with everybody else thinking you can shove weak-willed Carrie around. Give her orders and intimidate her into not checking on Joe.

"I don't give a rat's ass if the rest of you don't care what happens to him. I do, and I'm not backing down. I'm going down there and making sure he's all right, and none of you assholes are stopping me. Do you understand?"

Jazz grunted. "All too well. We've insulted you. But you know what? I don't care. You don't have any business going down there alone. You want to go? Fine. You'll go with me if I have to pick you up and put you in the damned Jeep myself."

He started toward her, but in a lightning-fast move, Carrie pulled a gun from her handbag and shot three times at his feet. He jumped back and held his hands up.

"Fine. I won't pick you up and put you in the Jeep myself. But—"

"But nothing," Carrie spat. "Move the damned Jeep and let me out of the driveway or I'm calling the police. I'll tell them what you just told me. It sounds a lot like a threat to kidnap, doesn't it?"

Jazz thought fast. He'd mistakenly believed taking charge in a firm manner was the way to go, but apparently this feisty woman was immune to it. He'd have to change his approach. Okay. Firm and take charge were out. Reasoning with her might work.

"All right, all right. But I want you to listen to me for five fucking minutes, and then if you still want to go down there by yourself, I won't stop you."

She kept the gun on him while she pulled her phone out of her handbag and glanced at it. "Your five minutes has started. You might want to start by explaining why you're so determined to go to Mexico and check on *my* stepfather. A man you've never laid eyes on in your life."

"Because Harlan's worried about him," Jazz said.

"Bullshit. Try again."

"Because he's an American citizen in a foreign country and may be in danger, and the government needs your cooperation."

"Another bullshit answer," she seethed. "The government could care less if a retired American has fallen ill. Clock's ticking, pal."

Well, hell. She wasn't buying his lies, and he couldn't tell her the truth without blowing his cover. "Will you at least talk to Harlan?"

"So he can lie for you? No. The only people I'm willing to talk to right now wear blue uniforms and badges, so if you don't move the damned Jeep, you'll be talking to them."

Shit. She meant every word. Persuasion wasn't working this morning. He'd have to try something else. He shot off a quick text to Harlan.

Carrie determined to go, call her.

He put his phone in his pocket and continued the stare-down.

It was hard to reconcile this woman to the stories he'd heard about Carrie Burke, the woman who'd let her boyfriend abuse her to the point Harlan had murdered him.

She held his gaze, clear-eyed and unafraid. She was going to go to Mexico to find Joe, and to hell with anybody or anything standing in her way.

Including him.

She wasn't the wimp they all made her out to be.

And damn if it didn't make his dick hard just thinking about what that meant.

ABOUT THE AUTHOR

Author of over forty romance novels, Emily Mims combined her writing career with a career in public education until leaving the classroom to write full time. The mother of two sons, she and her husband split their time between central Texas, eastern Tennessee, and overseas visiting their kids and grandchildren.

For relaxation Emily plays the piano, organ, dulcimer, and ukulele for two different performing groups, and even sings a little.

She says, "I love to write romances because I believe in them. Romance happened to me and it can happen to any woman—if she'll just let it."

Connect with Emily:

website: emilymims.com

IG: @mims_emily

TicTok:@emilywmims

FB: emily.mims.756

twitter: @emilymimsauthor

www.BOROUGHSPUBLISHINGGROUP.com

If you enjoyed this book, please write a review. Our authors appreciate the feedback, and it helps future readers find books they love. We welcome your comments and invite you to send them to info@boroughspublishinggroup.com. Follow us on TikTok, Twitter, and Instagram, and be sure to sign up for our newsletter for surprises and new releases from your favorite authors.

Are you an aspiring writer? Check out www.boroughspublishinggroup.com/submit and see if we can help you make your dreams come true.

Love podcasts? Enjoy ours at www.boroughspublishinggroup.com/podcast

www.ingramcontent.com/pod-product-compliance
Lightning Source LLC
Chambersburg PA
CBHW031332170626
46807CB00002B/656